DOUBLE DOWN TROUBLE

J. L. SALTER

Dingbat Publishing
Humble, Texas

DOUBLE DOWN TROUBLE
Copyright © 2018 by Jeffrey L. Salter
ISBN 978-1721273836

Published by Dingbat Publishing
Humble, Texas

All rights reserved. No part of this book may be reproduced in any form or by any means without written consent, excepting brief quotes used in reviews.

This is a work of fiction. Names, places, characters, and events are entirely the product of the author's imagination or are used fictitiously, and any resemblance to persons, living or dead, actual locals, events, or organizations is coincidental.

This book is licensed to the original purchaser only. Duplication or distribution via any means is illegal and a violation of International Copyright Law, subject to criminal prosecution and upon conviction, fines and/or imprisonment. No part of this book can be reproduced or sold by any person or business without the express permission of the publisher.

DEDICATION

―――✧―――

Carlos W. Colón
1953–2016

I FIRST MET Carlos as we both began graduate library school at LSU in September 1976. Over those forty years of friendship, we were also library colleagues for at least 25 years. For most of those four decades we encouraged each other's creative writing — and even collaborated on several projects — as well as occasionally golfing and playing cards together.

You didn't have to agree on everything to be a good friend of Carlos — he always sought (and usually found) some sort of common ground with anyone who gave him a chance. For example, Carlos was a huge fan of authors and music that I had no taste for. It didn't bother him that I didn't share affection for his favorites — and it never bothered me that Carlos didn't adore mine. That was the beauty of our friendship: we were compatible and complementary, without feeling any need to be identically inclined.

These days, politics harshly divides friends and even families. But in all those years we were friends, I don't recall discussing politics with Carlos and cannot say (now) where his political leanings rested. It didn't matter. We connected on the ground we *shared*.

Surely, there can be no better basis for friendship.

As a person, Carlos was honest, respectful, loyal, compassionate, generous, and kind. Even in the face of determined negativity and attack, he always took the high road.

At having this novel dedicated to him, I think Carlos would have smiled broadly. If souls in Heaven can be aware of such things, I hope he learns of this dedication.

Gosh, I miss my dear friend.

CHAPTER 1

A Sunday in mid-October

I WAS WASHING my hands in the restroom when a deafening blast hit me like a baseball bat to the head. As I worked my jaw to clear my ears, the unmistakable bursts of automatic weapons sent me to the floor. Shooters! Screams. Gunfire seemed to be coming from all over the building and possibly outside as well, but most specifically in the performance room I'd recently left. I huddled down behind the stall wall.

My security detail, both state troopers, had been uneasy about the layout of this historic building, and they'd disagreed on where to position themselves while I watched the performance. I was still too new in this high-stress job to have thought much about my safety team, but I surely needed them now.

Angry shouting. Heavy footsteps. At least one muffled voice. And people banging against the walls of the hallway. My only weapon was a tiny canister of chemical spray in my shoulder-strap purse, so I held my breath and waited to one side of the restroom door until that commotion passed by. Whoever they were, I didn't want to tangle with them.

And where had they come from? Surely not from the performance space.

Since the play selections had not overly impressed me, I'd mostly been watching others among our small, diverse audience. Besides the middle-aged man in an ill-fitting suit who'd kept checking his watch, I was most impressed by a female naval officer in full uniform bedecked in ribbons, and a thirty-something man wearing nice jeans and polished boots with what appeared to be an old army jacket. All three of them had looked out of place but only the naval officer appeared to be paying much attention to the play. The man with the bad suit had perched near the exit, while the handsome jeans guy sat in the far corner right next to a massive wooden podium that had been dragged out of the way of the actors.

Attendance at this event was by invitation only. The smattering of other individuals among our modest three dozen viewers were what I'd expect to be Greene County's society matrons, local politicians, and perhaps some business leaders. That explosion had surely injured everybody present in the performance room. Likely killed several.

Soon the rapid fire, now more distant, slowed to short bursts and then to single gunshots. Those final shots sounded selective and brutally deliberate. If I had remained in the audience, I'd likely be dead already. During a brief lull in the performance — for their set change — I'd visited the restroom so I could later quickly exit to our state police cruiser and head straight back to the city when this event was over. The anxious-looking man near the exit had gotten up shortly before I did, so perhaps he'd had a similar notion, though I hadn't seen him in the short hallway near the restrooms.

Focus, Julia!

I'd been to numerous safety workshops, but nothing had prepared me for what to do next. Only my instincts spoke up — *find your security detail*. But first I had to check on the playwright — my college friend, Pamela. It was mainly at her insistence that I'd rescheduled my sparse calendar in Nashville and arranged to spend a good chunk of Sunday 35 miles east supporting the arts on the top floor of Verdeville's historic office building, recently renovated into a municipal annex.

More noise and gunfire in other parts of the building and presumably outside on the street below. I flinched again. *Focus!*

After listening for any further sounds nearby, I slowly opened the restroom door and eased back toward the sizeable performance room. Through the smoke and clutter, I saw dozens of bodies, most riddled with bullets, and blood everywhere on the walls and floor. The visual shock was as horrible as the acrid smell and heavy smoke, but it was the terrified expressions on their faces that pierced my heart. I hurried to Pamela, partly covered by the director. Both showed multiple bullet wounds and neither had even the trace of a pulse.

Panic prevented grief from hitting me yet. Survival instinct said to keep moving and find my security team. No time to stop and figure out what had happened. Certainly no moment for an inventory, but it was clear that none of the three individuals I'd previously monitored were among these casualties. Perhaps the nervous man had never returned. But the female naval officer and the guy with the old olive drab jacket were also gone.

CHAPTER 2

If I'd been thinking, I would've called 9-1-1. But I wasn't... and didn't. *Get to safety.*

I hurried out of the body-littered ad hoc theatre and checked at the hallway, lightly streaked with blood along the floor. Somebody who'd passed by was injured but presumably still alive. Didn't see anyone in either direction, so I returned to the main central space to look for Trooper Todd. He was at his assigned station — well, his bullet-riddled body was. I knew Todd was dead before I covered the thirty feet to reach him.

Knelt beside him on the floor. No pulse or respiration — just a massive exit wound in the middle of his chest, a blank look of astonishment in his lifeless eyes, and a smaller entrance wound on his forehead. Shot in the back and then finished off from the front... at close range judging from the powder burns. My default thinking was not to touch anything else since this was a crime scene. But it seemed more like an active battle zone, so I grabbed Todd's pistol from his hand. Safety was off and the hammer was back. Plus, I knew from the smell it had been fired, so he'd clearly tried to get in some licks before he was mowed down from behind.

Whatever had occurred in this municipal annex was obviously connected to the other blasts and gunfire elsewhere on this east side of downtown Verdeville. But *what* had happened? Thus far, I'd seen nothing but the aftermath, so I didn't even know who the perpetrators were. Terrorists? Foreign invaders? Could've been anybody with access to explosives and automatic weapons — in other words, a long list of possible suspects.

More noise from the floors below, so I rose quickly — so fast that my head dizzied — and started down the hallway toward the primary exit.

"No!" hissed a frantic male whisper from somewhere behind me. "Not that way." It was the man in the old army jacket. Blood on his scalp and face, but he was moving with no apparent impediment and heading my direction. The barrel of my borrowed pistol had found his torso at the same time my eyes identified him.

"That's the way to the exit," I said.

He hurried over, trying to edge away from my line of fire. "Yeah, but they'll be watching that main door for stragglers." When he got within three feet of me, he said, "Let me have that gun."

"Not on your life." I stepped back a bit for more distance between us and re-centered the muzzle at his broad chest.

He brushed my barrel to one side and moved past me to the body of Todd. Grabbed two full magazines from a belt pouch and returned to me, pulling my elbow as he did. "If you're keeping the pistol, here's more ammo. I'm guessing we'll need it before this is over."

"What's going on?" I yanked away my arm. "Who are you?"

"You saw me. I was in the room for that play. Let's go."

"There were lots of people in that room. Maybe somebody connected to all this killing and destruction."

"Could be. But I'm not with them. Let's get out of here."

"What about the others?"

"Everybody's dead. All that's left in there are bullet holes and body parts."

As well I knew from my own rapid survey. "How did *you* get out alive?"

When he shook his head, evidently the pain reminded him to check his scalp wound. He grabbed a handkerchief from his back pocket and pressed it against the bloody area. "When that stun grenade came flying in, I ducked behind the massive speaker stand. The guys with guns either didn't see me or they assumed their bullets went through."

Stun grenade? "You got hit by something." I pointed to his head.

"Not a bullet. I must've snagged it inside the lectern." Then he extended both arms for a cursory inspection. "Hope I don't get any blood on this Ike jacket."

"Ike?"

"My grandfather's Eisenhower jacket from World War Two." He seemed more worried about the coat than his own head wound.

"What were you doing here to begin with?" I asked.

"Invited. I grew up with the director, and Rick is just as dead as the rest of them."

"I know. My friend who wrote the play was killed, too. But there were two other people."

He scratched his head on the opposite side of the wound. "I saw a guy near the exit who wasn't paying attention to the play. He left shortly before you did. You didn't seem interested either."

How'd he know that? "What about that woman in uniform?"

"Oh, the rear admiral?"

"Admiral?"

"Yeah," said the Ike jacket guy. "One star. It's what they call rear admiral, lower half."

"Wow. Didn't know the Navy had women that high up."

"Plenty of them now. But I didn't see her body, if that's what you mean. Maybe she got away."

"Could you hear anything from behind that podium?"

With a finger and thumb, he pinched the top of my gun barrel and again re-directed it from his torso.

I knew better — I'd handled guns before — but I wasn't exactly thinking straight.

"I heard shouting and scuffling," he said. "But mostly somebody stepping through the tumbles of chairs and bodies and finishing off anyone who was still moaning."

I tried to blot out my emotions. "Well, I heard what sounded like somebody being banged against the wall a few times in that short hallway right outside the restroom. Wonder if that was the officer."

"No telling," said Ike Jacket. "If she lived through all that, she might be in for worse later."

I shuddered. "What happened here? And what's still going on outside?"

"We can talk later." He pointed to the pistol. "Where's the rest of your security detail?"

He said it like he recognized me. "You know me?"

"You're from the state capitol. I've seen pictures."

"Probably during the campaign." I'd been nearly invisible since then.

"That's one way."

Caught me by surprise. "There's another?"

Ike didn't stop to explain. "So... where's your other troopers?"

"Only one more. Denny was stationed downstairs, at or near the building entrance."

"Hopefully he took cover somewhere. He'd be dead meat with bad guys moving in and out those main doors."

When we both heard a noise, Ike shoved me against the wall and looked out into the hallway. "Seems clear," he said. "Sorry about your upstairs trooper."

"Todd was a good man."

"Nothing we can do for him now. Or for our two friends in that other room." He swallowed hard. "Normally, if able to hide undetected and not actively being pursued, we'd be expected to shelter in place until help arrives." Then he shook his head slowly. "But we need to get out of here."

"To where?"

"Out. Away." He looked both directions again. "Fire exit should be the safest."

"I should call in first."

More gunfire elsewhere in the building... possibly the bottom floor.

"I'm not hanging around here while you yak on the phone." He grabbed me by my free arm and said, "Let's go. Quick."

I slung my bag's strap over my head so it rested on my opposite shoulder, then I stuffed the extra magazines inside. Kept the pistol out.

On our way, we saw other carnage and it was clear that nearly everybody in the building had already been killed or captured — though on a Sunday around noon, that was mainly our group upstairs and likely the county emergency office in the basement. When we reached an outside window, we peeked out to the street below and saw total chaos, dozens of men in orange jumpsuits, most waving guns.

"Prisoners," said Ike. "Likely on their way to or from the penitentiary in Nashville." He pointed to two huge, dark, unmarked, but heavily caged buses parked out front.

Thought I heard police car sirens in the distance, but wasn't certain. No sign of any living good guys, hostages or otherwise, near the annex building or outside the office structures across the street.

"We've got to get out of here," he said as he hustled me along a back corridor that seemed little used and toward what I assumed was an alley exit — maybe an unused delivery area.

"What about Trooper Denny at the entrance?"

"Most likely anybody in a law enforcement uniform is dead. But if he's alive, they've got him and he'll wish he was dead." Ike tugged again at my arm.

I pulled away. "I have to check."

After he scowled and cursed, Ike followed me as I led the way toward the other assigned position for my security detail. No trooper at the main exit, though several of the orange jumpsuits were standing around and looking unsure what to do next. After we backed away quietly, I spotted Denny, motionless on the floor near the single elevator, away from the convicts at the main doors. He'd probably been on his way up to me when he was gunned down. Even from fifteen feet away, I could see they'd also fired at his head, likely guessing he wore body armor. Tears burned down my cheeks, but I didn't make a sound.

"You stay here," said Ike. "I'll check him." Hurrying over, he searched for a pulse, then shook his head as he quickly eyed me. Then he unlatched Denny's heavy belt rig, including the weapon and cuffs, and carefully clutched them to his chest.

Ike bumped me to get me moving as he trotted down the long narrow hallway toward the side or rear exit — I couldn't determine which direction it was.

Puzzled that I hadn't done this before even though it had flitted through my brain, I whipped my cell phone out of my purse and dialed 9-1-1.

"What are you doing?" asked Ike, leaning his ear closely.

"Calling emergency. That office is supposed to be in the basement of this building."

Just then a gruff voice answered. "Uh, hello. This is, um, 9-1-1. Who are you?"

Ike had been listening. "Hang up," he hissed.

I covered the mouthpiece and whispered, "Why?"

He grabbed the phone and disconnected the call. "That wasn't the real dispatcher."

"And how could you possibly know?"

"The assigned folks could see your name and number in their display. That guy didn't know where your call came from."

"So, who was he?"

"Probably one of whoever's taken over this part of downtown." Ike's eyes were wild as they connected with mine and he looked around urgently. He grabbed my shoulders and shoved us both tightly into a small intersecting hallway. "That means they've taken over the emergency control center, too."

I struggled to get away from his strong grip. I wasn't actually afraid of Ike harming me, but he was simply too close. "Slow down. We need to contact *somebody*."

"Later. Right now we need to get out of this building and away from downtown. Whatever's happening is most likely localized."

How could he know that? Or even guess?

CHAPTER 3

―――♦―――

THOUGH HE SEEMED to divine my questions, the man I knew only as Ike explained nothing as he stared into my eyes, seemingly scanning for ideas. "What kind of vehicle did you come in?"

I described the state police cruiser.

"Have you got a set of keys?"

"No. Only Todd and Denny had keys."

"Wish you'd mentioned that when we were across the building."

You didn't ask.

"And I should've taken his collar mic, too." He nodded in the direction of Denny's lifeless body, on the floor in front of the distant elevator. "I don't think we can get back over there without being seen."

"Nobody else is down there," I protested.

"Listen!" He clutched my shoulder harshly. "In the hallways and coming down the stairs."

He was probably right, but all I heard was footsteps and shouts. The inside shooting had finally stopped a few moments ago. After the shock of seeing my dead friends, I'd forced myself to tune out much of the additional gunfire.

"Where's the cruiser?"

"On the side. Parked in the alley. Unless Denny moved it."

"Which side? North or south?"

I pointed to my left.

"South." His head jerked around again and he shoved us into a short hallway to a warren of small offices. "We can't risk going that direction. Even if we had the keys."

"Why not? What are you talking about?"

"Look. I'm trying to keep you in one piece, but I need you to focus. First, we exit this trap. Next, we clear downtown. Only then do we stop to yak about it. Right now I need you to move and move fast."

"Where are we going?"

"Out. Away. North."

"Nothing north of this little town but a few neighborhoods and lots of forest land."

"Woods mean safety right now." His eyes fixed mine again. "You're gonna have to move fast and trust me."

"Why? You're a total stranger."

"Not really. We've met before, Julia Temple."

He'd used my maiden name, so he was savvy enough to know I'd reclaimed it after divorcing Arnold Bane. "Met when? Where?"

"No time to explain now. Let's go."

"Why should I listen to you? I don't even know you."

"You don't know those guys in orange jumpsuits either, and you don't want to." He started hustling us toward an exit door on what must have been the north side of the building.

"At least tell me your name."

"Doc Holliday."

"You're kidding."

"The first part is a nickname I can't shake." Holliday groaned. He strapped on Trooper Denny's rig and, miraculously, it fit without adjustments... though a little loose on Holliday. "Let's move. Now."

Holliday was scraping along the left side wall, and he'd motioned me to go along the right. I shoved the phone back into my shoulder-strap purse and started to uncock the pistol so I could stow it also.

"Better keep that out."

Hurrying to keep as nearly abreast of him as I could, I nearly asked why but then thought better of it.

He just glared. "You know how to use it?"

"Yeah. I've trained on the Beretta 92." It would have been more accurate to say I'd practiced with that model a few times. There'd been no formal training, but I knew how it worked. I'd only shot at paper targets, however, and those only at the state police facility.

"Good. Keep it cocked and locked."

I eased down the hammer, then flipped the safety on. Pulled back the slide enough to confirm a round was already chambered, then switched the safety off again. Cocked the hammer. *Ready to fire.*

Holliday motioned with his hand. "And stop pointing it at me."

"I wish you'd slow down and tell me..."

"Shhh." He halted suddenly as we neared the exit door. "Hug that wall and let me take a quick peek outside."

I didn't do any hugging, but I sort of flattened.

Holliday opened the door just a crack and peered outside. Then he put his ear to that same crack. "More gunfire outside. But it sounds a few blocks away and so far it's all to the south."

What's the big deal about the south? Only thing I remembered over there was a huge parking lot for most of the people in this courthouse annex complex. "So what do we do?"

"Like I said, north toward the woods."

"No," I replied. "I'll go to the edge of downtown with you, but I'm stopping there and contacting somebody." Didn't feel like trucking through the residential neighborhoods and forestland with a total stranger — even though he claimed we'd met before. Anybody could pretend he was a rescuer.

"Okay. Good revision to the plan. But right now, we need to get to safety."

"Those prisoners we saw running loose — where are they from?"

"Prison." Holliday's face was much too grim to have been attempting humor. "Riverbend State Prison in Nashville — it's maximum security. These guys are probably on their way to, or from, some federal prison, maybe in Memphis or Knoxville."

"Buses don't just drive into Verdeville with hundreds of convicts."

"Not that many," said Holliday, aggravatingly taking my estimate literally. "Probably a max of two dozen in each bus, so let's say a total of four dozen convicts."

Somehow that was not in the least reassuring. "What is all this about?"

"Later. If we live through the next five minutes, I'll tell you everything I know or can guess."

I was wearing a light gray executive suit, and he grabbed both the wool-blend jacket and my silk blouse between my neck and shoulder, took a deep breath, and propelled us both through the door. "Quiet and quick. Go."

My adrenaline had me moving but I made a better stride after he finally let go of my clothing. Well, not much of a stride with a tight, knee-length skirt and three-inch heels. When we reached a row of parked cars, he hunkered down and pulled me with him. My skirt nearly split and my bare knees scraped the pavement. More gunshots in the distance, but they appeared to be from the other side of the building we'd just left. A few more sounds inside it, however — glass breaking and more shouts.

Holliday had been visually scouting the area. "You know much about this side of town?" he asked breathlessly.

I told him what little I knew, but I'd never lived in Greene County and had only visited a few times. *Not exactly a destination.* We were three or four blocks north of the main street strip, and there wasn't much on this portion of downtown but some two- and three-story office structures and apartment buildings. Sprinkled among them were a few stores, many closed for the past few years, since I-40 had drawn away much of the former downtown retail.

"Are these buildings occupied?" He pointed toward the multi-floor office structures.

"Probably not on Sundays." The nearest churches were on the west side of downtown. "Didn't you say you and the director grew up here?"

"Not downtown. And quite a few years back."

Wondered how many years — he looked about my age, or slightly younger.

"What about those others?" He indicated the apartment buildings.

"Probably at least half of them would be home. You think they'd help us?"

"We don't have time to find out, but I doubt they'd be much help even if they were home." He kept looking around and seemed to try to slow his breathing. "We need a better place to conceal ourselves, but it'd be nice to be able to see what's going on, too."

I pointed to one of the nearby three-story apartment buildings with a flat roof.

"Nah. Don't want to get trapped up there." Holliday looked over his shoulder. "Need some green space with trees."

I had no intention of playing Tarzan with a guy I didn't know. "Trees?"

"Not to climb. It'll be good cover while we plan our escape route. Wish we knew what those guys have in mind."

I could only shrug. I didn't even know what Holliday had in mind.

"I remember a little park just beyond those buildings." He pointed toward what I guessed was north.

"How little?" I asked.

"Used to be a few square blocks, as I recall."

"Still not sure why you think we'll be safe there."

Without explaining his rationale, Holliday pointed again. "We turn left just behind that building and the park's nearest corner is maybe three or four blocks north."

So many conflicting impulses in my whirring brain and churning guts. Escape the convicts — sure. But trust some stranger who claimed he knew me? My antennae were quivering. "Look, you said earlier that we've met before."

He nodded. "Not like a handshake meeting, but I've encountered you."

Then why don't I remember? "Not a bad encounter, I hope."

"No. Not bad at all." He grinned nervously as his eyes swept the area to our south. "Quite good, in fact."

I took a deep breath, which I'd needed for the past many minutes. "You can't leave me hanging there."

"Let's just say I thought you were the most beautiful young woman I'd ever seen in real life and I swore that one day we'd have another chance to meet properly."

That made me gulp hard. "Wonder how come we didn't."

"Because you married that schmuck Bane."

CHAPTER 4

AH YES, ARNOLD Bane — the handsome, personable college boy I'd married before I realized he was too immature and self-centered to maintain an adult relationship. Before I could retrieve any further thoughts about my ex, however, Holliday grabbed my shoulder again.

"Okay. We keep to the inside of the sidewalk and don't cross the street 'til I say." He locked onto my eyes again. "Ready?" After I nodded, he took a deep breath, exhaled noisily, and said, "Now." And he took off.

In heels and skirt, I was quite a few paces behind. We covered those 400 feet in two seconds flat. Well, it was pretty fast.

Then Holliday dropped to a crouch behind a low set of bushes and pulled me down beside him. He pointed back toward Taylor, the avenue we'd just crossed. "That's one of the streets to the park."

Something looked familiar and I nodded, panting roughly. "North, a few blocks."

He rose up enough to see over the bushes, then back down where he was level with my face again. "Across to that next street and then north 'til we can tuck behind that big sign. Okay?" When I nodded, he said, "Ready, now." And he sprinted west along a full block of Ash Street, paused for me to catch up, and then jogged north on Fillmore Avenue.

I was slowing down. Even in jogging shorts and sneakers, this would be rough, but in those shoes, I was breaking a dozen laws of podiatry. Thought about removing them, but I'd seen too many movies with barefoot heroines. *Nope.*

Holliday was already crouched behind the sign at Hickory and Fillmore and waving me in.

As I covered the remaining few feet, he was urgently scanning to the south. "Don't think they spotted us."

I hadn't seen many orange outfits since we'd left the municipal annex building. So maybe they were concentrated on the south of downtown, as Holliday had assumed. I noticed a puzzled expression on his sweaty face.

"My friend Rick — did you meet the director?" asked Holliday. "Well, he mentioned that the production's complete cast and crew were waiting in Knoxville for tomorrow's larger performance of even more selections."

"Yeah, that's what Pamela told me." I wondered why Holliday was pausing to be reflective when he'd been pushing me to *move move move*.

"I was just wondering if this complete show would later be on Broadway, as they'd announced, or does a tragedy like this just..." He trailed off.

I figured the show would go on, but somehow I didn't feel like verbalizing it. They'd probably use understudies to replace those five actors killed this afternoon, but I couldn't guess who would take over as director. After watching Holliday's silent, shocked face for another moment, I carefully put down the pistol and pulled out my phone.

My movement abruptly ended his reverie. "What are you doing?"

"I need to call somebody. Report what's happening."

"Believe me, they already know."

"Who would already know, and how? Everything's happened in a matter of minutes. If they took over the 9-1-1 office like you said, then maybe nobody knows anything."

"They knew it almost while it was happening."

Impossible. "What is all this about anyhow?"

"Possibly the worst prison break in Tennessee history. Two full busloads of convicts." Holliday checked all directions around us. "I saw them when I came up to the annex."

"They must have arrived after I'd already entered the building."

"So how come you reached the performance room after I did?" he asked.

I shrugged. "Todd and Denny couldn't agree on which positions to take. Plus, I'd stopped to chat with the playwright." Thinking of Pamela made me choke up again.

"Well, those buses were locked up when I went by. Well guarded, too. Driver and monitor in the separate front cage. Two armed guards outside of each bus — one front and one back. Hard to imagine somebody overpowering eight guards."

"Who could do that?"

"Whoever routed them from the interstate to downtown Verdeville."

Prison buses don't just get re-routed. "Why?"

"Maybe somebody important wanted out of prison before he got transferred to the other facility." His eyes never stopped moving, checking all directions. "Or could be somebody on the outside wanted to do something downtown and needed a huge distraction to get it done."

"Nobody in their right mind would set loose some four dozen hardened convicts on the population of downtown Verdeville. How could they control them?"

"Good point. Maybe they started out trying to free just a handful, but other guys overpowered the ones letting out their select group."

Incredible. "So what's your plan now?"

"Not sure, but we can figure it out later. Biggest thing is to get some distance from those orange guys."

"Wait a second." Maybe he was trying to help, but maybe he wanted me in the woods for some other reason. "Who are you, anyway?"

"Doc Holliday. Told you. Call me Doc."

"Not your name. *What* are you?"

"Just a former resident who returned from Clarksville for a quick visit and stumbled into a bad scene."

My face must have been totally blank.

"We can iron all that out later. Right now, I'm hoping to be a survivor. What about you?"

Couldn't think of an appropriate reply to a pointless question, so I picked up my phone again.

"Who are you calling?"

"At the very least, I need to report in. Find out what the governor's office knows and what he's doing about it."

"Is Governor Ampersand good to work with?"

I sighed heavily. "I hardly work with him at all."

"How come? I thought the governor and lieutenant governor were a team."

"So did I, but it seems I'm treated more like a distraction than a partner."

"Seriously? Because you're an attractive woman?"

"Partly." Trying to ignore his compliment, I eyed Holliday... um, Doc critically. "But also because he was really close with my dad at one point."

"Jonathan Temple. Former U.S. senator. Right?"

I nodded. "Tell me more about this encounter we supposedly had, and why it might seem fuzzy to me." *Fact is, I don't remember it at all.*

"Later. When we're clear."

"You keep saying later, but I need to know who I'm running with." I'd always been taught to go with my gut instincts and they were still warning me about throwing in with strangers.

Doc groaned, anxiously checked to the south, and hurriedly explained. When he'd been in high school, his class had gone to Nashville to see the state capital and also visit the home office of U.S. Senator Jonathan Temple. "When we got there, the senator had been summoned back to D.C. for an emergency vote on some important bill."

"Dad got called back to Washington a lot." I still didn't remember meeting a teenaged Doc Holliday. "But what does your field trip have to do with me?"

"You were there... in the office."

"I interned for him, but only during the summers." I was flattered that my clerical presence had made such an impression on a younger Doc and asked him why.

"Better not say." He strained his neck to search for the distant orange jumpsuits.

"Well, at least give me a hint."

"Okay. Suffice it to say our current lieutenant governor is a total fox with killer legs." He paused to see my reaction, which was a slight blush. "And still as foxy now as you were fourteen years ago."

CHAPTER 5

TRYING TO IGNORE the flattery, which I assumed was mostly Doc's nervous flirtation, I had my phone out again and was ready to press speed dial for the private number of Gov. Ampersand's secretary, Charise. No point in trying to reach my own secretary, because Helen was on vacation with her husband and two kids.

"If you get through, what are you going to tell the governor?" asked Doc.

"Two buses of convicts loose in downtown Verdeville, killing people and presumably taking at least a few hostages."

"I'm betting he already knows that much."

"How could he, if the 9-1-1 office was taken over?"

"They have emergency protocols in place now," he replied. "Word gets out instantly when things go bad. It's all part of the sophisticated Homeland Security apparatus."

I wondered how my cryptic companion knew all that, but didn't need to inquire because he read my puzzled expression.

"Many cities now have gunfire detection monitors which can both detect and localize the source area of the shots," he explained.

"Even a small town like Verdeville?"

"Everybody's hooked up these days, except the most rural, isolated, unpopulated areas. Surveillance cameras, building sensors, reconnaissance drones, satellite images..."

"Okay, okay. I get it. Maybe they already know, but I've still got to do something."

"Yeah," he said, motioning north with his head. "Get clear. Find safety. We're nuts to sit here yakking."

"I have a duty to try to help." It sounded corny to repeat that under the new state constitution, I was a publicly elected state official. Formerly, my position was selected from the state senators.

"If you stick around here, you'll be a casualty or a hostage... and that won't help anybody." He checked his watch, likely calculating how many minutes it had been since all hell broke loose. "Wonder when the troops will arrive?"

All of a sudden, it hit me — during my 24 months in office, I'd never experienced a security briefing any more specific than what the state capitol's pool reporters received. "What kind of, uh, police response can we expect for something like this?"

"Hard to say," replied Doc. "A lot has changed since Homeland Security was formed."

"What if these are *state* prisoners attacking this municipality? Wouldn't that be handled by Tennessee officials?"

"I doubt Tennessee has ever dealt with anything like this," said Doc as he continued to monitor the streets in three directions. No traffic whatsoever — typical Sunday downtown. "I assume each prison has a contingency plan for escapes. But most of those scenarios likely involve internal measures within various areas of the prison complex."

"A federal response team would have a lot more resources," I added, "but presumably they'd also be farther away."

"Right. But here's the big wrinkle — what happened just now was a large scale escape during transport *between* prisons."

"I think I saw a movie about that." I realized we'd drifted off the point at hand. "Well, all these guys got loose somehow and *somebody* needs to round them up."

Doc quickly scanned the streets again. "If it were my call, I guess I'd mobilize the Tennessee National Guard. Is there still a local company in Verdeville?"

"Not for several years. I'm pretty sure the former armory is just a community center now," I said. "I remember my father fought to allow Greene County to keep its local guard unit." *But he lost.*

"I would've thought your father swung enough weight to do anything he wanted... I mean, he was a senator for so long that everybody down to kindergarten knew his name."

I ignored half of his question — the answer was politics. "The cynics say Dad's name is the only reason I was elected."

"They have a point… name recognition. Speaking of elections, I thought the lieutenant governor was selected by the senate. How did your name get in the hopper?"

Doesn't anybody read newspapers any more? "That changed with the recent overhaul of the state constitution. The senators have enough to do, and I'd assumed the revised lieutenant governor's position would become more of a functioning executive partner with Ampersand."

Suddenly Doc eyed his watch again and began shaking his head. "We're wasting valuable time here, and it's too dangerous out on the street." He got to his feet but was still hunched over. "Now let's get to that park and figure out the best direction to head from there."

"No." I gulped. "I mean, I'm not going."

He looked stunned.

Maybe Doc's used to people doing whatever he says.

"Look, we just barely managed to escape kidnapping, death, or maybe something worse at the hands of four dozen crazed convicts, and now you want to double down? Wasn't that enough trouble and terror for one morning?"

"If you need to clear out, I guess I understand, but I'm obligated at least to try and help."

"Help what? Help who?"

"Well, for one thing, I need to communicate with Ampersand and see what resources he has heading this way."

Doc crouched back down, his feet flat and his butt nearly touching the pavement. "Make it fast."

I started to tell him he was free to go but swallowed those words. It would be a comfort to have him around. My own secretary knew I was in Verdeville, but Helen was on vacation out of state and not dealing with office matters. I'd turned my phone off during the performance and assumed somebody from the governor's office would have been trying to reach me. But my phone had not rung since I'd turned it back on to make that quickly aborted 9-1-1 call.

Doc watched impatiently as I phoned the governor's office. I reached Kayla, his secretary's intern, and got a breathless, distracted response.

"Where's the governor's secretary?" I asked.

"Charise is with the governor. They left me to cover the phones here."

"Have you guys been trying to reach me?"

"Uh, no."

"Why not, Kayla?"

A long pause in which I detected mortified panic. "I, uh, wasn't told to contact you."

I felt like screaming, but that would only rattle Kayla further. "I should be on the call list."

"The governor left only a few specific instructions," she protested. "You know how he is."

Yeah, I knew. *Doesn't use any initiative unless it directly benefits him.* "Well, I'm over here in Verdeville..."

"Verdeville?" she screeched. "That's where the big wreck happened."

"It's not a wreck, Kayla. It's two empty prison buses and four dozen convicts roaming around this little downtown."

"That's all anybody's talking about over here..."

"Well, I need to get into that conversation," I interjected. "Is the governor available?"

"No. He's at the crisis room in the basement."

"Do cell phones work down there?"

Her voice was querulous. "I'm not sure."

"Okay, can you patch me through?"

"I don't know." She sounded on the verge of tears. "I've never done this before. I'm confused. I'm alone here, dang it."

"Put it on speaker," said Doc. "I need to hear."

I did. "You're on speaker now. My companion is Doc Holliday — he was also at the performance. Now calm down, Kayla." I tried to think of something she could do with confidence. "Grab an intern or somebody."

"I *am* the intern!"

"Well, find a runner to send down to the crisis room. Tell the governor nearly fifty criminals have escaped from two buses that were presumably en route to, or from, Riverbend Prison but stopped over in Verdeville for a reason I'm not aware of. Once here, we're assuming they were let loose by somebody waiting for them... and it's logical those same individuals were responsible for creating that bogus emergency. Tell him that I was on site to attend a play. Presently, I'm on Hickory and Fillmore, a few blocks north of Main Street in Verdeville. I'm armed and safe at the moment. I have an armed civilian companion, but both Todd and Denny are..." My sobs finished the sentence.

"Both troopers are *dead*?" Kayla sounded near hysterics. She was friends with Denny's daughter.

I collected myself enough to continue. "There are dozens of citizens we've seen dead, and presumably many others, including the bus guards. My companion thinks a few guards and other individuals could be still alive as hostages. One of the possible hostages is a female admiral."

"Admiral? Like in the Navy?"

"Yeah... one star. Rear admiral, lower half," interjected Doc.

"What's a Navy officer doing at a small play in Verdeville?"

"No idea, but she really stuck out. That's probably why they took her hostage instead of killing her along with everybody else."

"Assuming she's still alive," added Doc.

"Call somebody in the Navy and find out which female admiral she is. It could be important."

"How would they know?"

Doc pulled the phone his way slightly. "No admiral or general goes anywhere without notifying a dozen people."

I took a deep breath and tried to sound like I knew what I was doing. "Listen carefully, Kayla. Get word to the governor and get back to me immediately. I need to know what resources he's sending, where they're coming from, and who's going to be their on-scene coordinator."

Doc interrupted me. "Be sure that coordinator knows we're here and has a way to get to you."

I repeated that to Kayla. "Now read that back and let's be sure you've got everything." She did and I made a minor correction. "I'm switching my phone to vibrate so we don't have any sudden noise in case that becomes a problem later. If I don't answer immediately, call again in five minutes unless I've called you back in the meantime. Got it?"

"I think so." She didn't sound too certain.

"Are we clear, Kayla?"

"Yeah. But why don't you just get out of there?"

Doc had been listening to most of this and edged even closer to hear my reply.

"I've been crouching here behind this sign trying to remember roughly how many citizens live in these apartments between Hickory and Ash streets."

"I doubt their landlord even knows," said Kayla. "But how could you possibly have even a clue? I thought you were raised in Nashville."

"True, but I've just remembered who some of these people are."

Doc's voice was in one ear and Kayla's in my other ear — and both responded at the same time. "Who?"

"I was here for a tour and ribbon-cutting last summer when this former office building was renovated into apartments and reopened for the first time as living spaces."

"So?" said Doc.

"This was a pilot project where rents are stabilized and mostly subsidized with federal and state funds."

"For who?" asked Kayla.

"For fixed income seniors, many of whom also have significant medical issues. Assisted living."

"Good Lord!" said Kayla.

Doc groaned. "Terrific."

There was a long silence on Kayla's end. "Uh, the governor's probably going to ask me what you have in mind."

"Don't know yet. First I have to find out how many seniors are in this building and how mobile they are."

"This is nuts, Julia." Doc sputtered. "You can't parade a few dozen old folks on walkers down Pierce Avenue with all those killers loose a block away. They'll be used for target practice."

"Maybe we're lucky and most of these residents are visiting relatives somewhere else," I said, though those hopeful words sounded hollow even to me.

"You need to get out of there, Mizz Temple," said Kayla. "And if the governor was standing right here, he'd tell you the same thing."

Doc was nodding.

No, he wouldn't. "If Governor Ampersand was in my shoes, he'd do exactly what I'm going to try."

"Which is?" prompted Kayla.

"Can't wait to hear this," said Doc with more acid than it needed.

"We're going to help protect those old folks in any way possible."

Doc exhaled noisily. "That's crazy."

Kayla was silent, but I knew her jaw had dropped to the desk. I'd seen that expression before when we'd learned the vice president was in town for an unscheduled visit after a horribly destructive tornado.

"Kayla, you relay everything to the governor and get back to me. Be sure that whoever's coming has my number and location. Ground zero is the..." I backed up enough to read the sign, "...Elderwood Apartments."

"No, ground zero is the municipal office annex we just left," said Doc, "and two prison buses parked right outside."

I had to tune him out. "Oh, one more thing. Be sure the governor knows that we're pretty certain some people are still alive as hostages. And don't forget to track down that admiral's name."

"Okay." Kayla's voice sounded weak and small.

"I'm counting on you, Kayla." I waited a second and then said, "Bye." I switched my phone to vibrate and stowed it in my heavy shoulder bag.

"Oh, brother," said Doc. "You can't be serious about hauling those old people away from downtown."

"Until the cavalry arrives, I'm going to do whatever can be done to protect them. If you're willing to help, I'd appreciate it. But if you're not, then give me Denny's weapon and ammo... and take off." That heavy belt also had cuffs and a Tazer.

"You're serious about staying?"

Yeah, doubling down on my troubles. "Dead serious."

CHAPTER 6

I COULDN'T ASSESS the deep frown on my new companion's otherwise handsome face. "So are you with me or not?"

After checking north, he fingered the belt rig he'd borrowed from the late Trooper Denny. For a second I thought Doc was going to unbuckle and remove it... then vamoose. Instead, he just slumped down to the pavement and groaned again. "Okay, what's your plan?"

"Thanks." I'm certain my relief showed. "First, we get into the Elderwood Apartments. They have a state-of-the-art central station on the main floor that acts as a check-in and check-out — among other things — so somebody always knows the whereabouts of each resident."

"So we can quickly figure out who's home," noted Doc. "And if they're all away visiting relatives, we can clear out from downtown and get to safety."

"You'd better count on several residents being present," I replied. "I'm sure many don't even have family nearby."

Just as he looked like he was about to cross his fingers, Doc cocked an ear and whispered, "Hear that?"

I hadn't.

Then he rose up and sprinted to the access road which cut south, about halfway along Hickory, between Fillmore and Pierce, where he stopped to wait on me. Once I arrived, out of breath, he loped to the north edge of the apartment building. By that point, I'd nearly collapsed. Taking a deep breath, he peered around the corner toward the south. Jerking back his head quickly, he groaned.

"What was it?" I asked between heaving pants.

"Several more orange suits holding what look like automatic rifles — but I'm hoping they're semi-auto — and roaming aimlessly."

"They've been doing that since we first spotted them."

"Yeah, but now they're heading toward the courthouse, apparently."

"Why are they still downtown?" I asked. "Don't escaped convicts usually scatter and vanish?"

Doc squinted his eyes like he had a migraine. "Good point. And it looks like most of them *have* already disappeared. There's got to be some reason for those guys to hang around and risk getting caught."

"Maybe they're the ones with the hostages."

"Could be," replied Doc. "But I'd expect those hostage keepers would be clustered in a highly defendable position while they wait for the federal negotiators to arrive."

"Any guesses how many convicts are involved with the hostages?" I gulped. "I mean, assuming they're still alive."

"Wild guess — a dozen at the most. And probably just the core group responsible for the bus re-routing." Then he shrugged. "Of course, that's purely speculation."

"So let's say a dozen remain with the hostages, either in the annex or if they're moving to the courthouse," I summarized. "And suppose half or more — maybe two dozen escapees — have already boogied out of here. What are those other guys doing, hanging around in downtown Verdeville?"

"We don't know who we're dealing with," replied Doc. "If these are hard-core murderers and rapists, they might believe they have some business to tend to before they high-tail it out of town."

My guts chilled over. The senior facility could logically be next.

"Look, we need to speed things up. Let's get inside, check that electronic sign-out panel, and see if anybody's home that we have to babysit."

"If the bad guys are approaching the front side, we'll have to slip in the back."

He grunted, then looked both ways. "Let's go."

I did, this time without waiting for his lead. We actually hit the rear door at about the same time and sort of fell together, breathing heavily. It felt weird being that close to a strange man — almost an embrace, though intimate only in proximity. Adrenaline and exertion had certainly blocked any possibility of romantic yearnings. Yet I did have a good memory...

"Locked," he said, as though it surprised him.

"Of course it is. Part of their high-tech security," I explained. "They gave me a full hour-long tour of this facility before we cut the ribbon last year."

"Hope you remember everything you saw," he said, breathing heavily. "Because we're gonna need every edge we can find."

I pressed the buzzer, obscurely placed, though not completely hidden.

"Elderwood Apartments," said a semi-pleasant voice. "Is this a delivery?"

"No, not a delivery. It's an emergency and we're here to help."

The intercom voice rose in pitch. "A what? Say again, please."

"Buzz us in. Your building's in the path of several escaped convicts — and it could be their next goal. We're here to help."

"Uh...."

"Lady, you open this door right now," interjected an agitated Doc Holliday. "You could trot to the front windows and see those armed thugs for yourself, except we don't have that much time."

The door buzzed and Doc yanked it open. We both tumbled through at the same time and that door slammed behind us. About eight feet farther, a second locked door buzzed and we both jerked it open. I remembered enough of the layout to lead the way around a corner to their central station, where we found an astonished middle-aged woman standing at her console and sputtering.

"We don't have time to explain right now, but a lot of dangerous convicts, most of them armed, are roaming downtown and several most likely heading this way," I said. "So we need you to cooperate."

"Convicts? In Verdeville?" Her mouth formed other syllables but none made sense other than to convey her panic and disbelief. "Don't escaped convicts just skedaddle?"

"Usually they do," answered Doc. "But we believe some are staying behind with several hostages — maybe as many as nine or ten."

"And a handful are out on the streets, presumably looking for trouble," I added. "Ma'am, do you recognize me?"

As the employee nodded slowly, Doc quickly added, "She's the lieutenant governor and we need your complete cooperation pronto."

Another nod as she plopped down into her rolling chair.

"What's your name, ma'am?" I asked.

She pointed to her name tag. "Heather. What do you want me to do?"

After two years in my position, suddenly someone was looking to me for answers… and I hesitated.

"Okay, Heather," said Doc, stepping in. "Be sure all those exterior doors are locked, give us a list of every resident on the premises this afternoon, contact all the able-bodied residents and get them moving down here to a secure inside room, and send somebody to all the individuals who need assistance to get them rolling. Got it?"

Writing notes almost as quickly as Doc had rattled off those orders, Heather nodded numbly and began pressing buttons on her console.

He'd covered everything I was going to say, but I had hoped to make it sound gentler somehow. From Doc, it sounded like the final puff on a last cigarette before the firing squad members pulled their triggers.

Finally I spoke up. "Be sure to call the Elderwood supervisor or owner and let them know the situation here."

Doc nodded his approval.

In a surprisingly calm voice, Heather was quickly on the intercom telling all the residents to immediately congregate in the cafeteria, but also urged them not to panic. "After we've collected everyone who's mobile," she explained to us, "we'll send back for those unable to move by themselves."

When Doc positioned his hand and fingers like a telephone, Heather made her call to whomever needed to know their Elderwood facility was in the path of a heavily armed tornado. Then Doc dashed to the bank of front windows, closed all the blinds, and peered out from the edge.

I joined him, though at the other edge of that same window bank.

He pointed through the thick glass. "That huge, tall building across those streets and over a block is the Greene County courthouse."

Easily recognizable. I nodded. I imagined it was also under attack, but not from the full swarm of orange which had occupied the annex where we'd been. I pictured them more as a small patrol.

"Who would you figure is in there?"

I had to guess creatively. "On a Sunday? Nobody working except maybe janitorial staff. Unless the police needed an emergency warrant and coaxed an agreeable judge to appear. No valuables to speak of." Then I thought of something. "Does this courthouse have a jail?"

"Not certain, but I don't believe so," he replied. "I think I recall reading that the court's holding cells moved to downtown's new police station, several blocks west."

"So it won't take that orange patrol long to check out the courthouse and turn their attention to other buildings more attractive for looting."

"If looting is what they have in mind. Likely there's still a drug store downtown somewhere," he offered. "But they'll never get into a bank that's closed."

From the direction of the distant annex building, another cluster of orange prison uniforms appeared, visible when they crossed a street we could see down — Pierce Avenue. At least half a dozen convicts were heading in our general direction and most were armed. "Where'd they get all those guns?"

"Don't know," replied Doc. "Don't plan to ask them either." Then he thought for a second. "I've already seen a lot more weapons than those eight guards would've had with them."

"Meaning...?"

"Whoever routed them here also already had a stash of weapons and ammo. Plus, I don't think routine bus guards would've been carrying stun grenades, so the local coordinator must've brought his own."

"Why did they pick Verdeville?" I asked, as elderly residents began to emerge from the adjacent elevator and two main hallways. Most regarded us cautiously as they hobbled toward the cafeteria.

Doc scowled as he considered the matter. "It's close to the interstate, but far enough away that the gunfire and explosions wouldn't be heard from there." Then his fingers moved back and forth like vehicles on a road. "Depending on which direction they were heading, this might have been the first stop after Nashville... or the last place *before* Nashville."

"That's another reason Verdeville doesn't make sense — it's so close to Nashville," I added. "Only thirty-some miles away. Didn't they figure Nashville would send a heavy law enforcement response?"

"Maybe they thought they could neutralize this 9-1-1 center before anybody got word out."

"But we already know the governor and his people found out."

"Yeah, so these convicts screwed up. The Homeland Security network must have alerted state and probably feds as soon as the first shot was heard."

"Thank goodness for that network. But do you think the bad guys know about it?"

"Possibly not. Which could explain why they're taking the time to drift around looting places."

Heather got off the phone, presumably with someone upstairs, and said everybody was either in the cafeteria or on their way. Then she punched a few console buttons and left her station to head to that safe room herself.

I faced Doc again. "That's why you think they're heading this way? Valuables?"

"Can't think of any other reason," he replied. "They know old people have stuff worth stealing."

"Even in assisted living apartments?"

"Absolutely. Jewelry, expensive watches, medicines, and probably cash."

"So this Elderwood building is definitely their target?" I asked as I pointed to the orange jumpsuits, over two blocks distant, having turned a corner and now clearly heading our way.

"You can bet on it. And unless they stop to loot those houses over there, they could be here in a few minutes. So let's get ready."

CHAPTER 7

I GULPED. THERE wasn't much time to get everybody organized, even though most residents had already trudged past us and headed toward the cafeteria, which doubled as their storm shelter. Some wheeled by in chairs, either motorized or manual. "Of course, we've been assuming there are at least two distinct groups of bad guys," I reminded Doc. "The ones who planned this and the others who escaped through collateral action."

"If I'd been planning a major breakout like this, I think I would've picked a spot like Crossville instead," he said. "They're on a major U.S. highway that goes the full height of the state, including south to Chattanooga."

"So we're back to *why Verdeville?*" I said. "And except for the 9-1-1 office, why that annex building?"

He shook his head slowly. "None of this makes sense. I have to assume the play production was a fly in the ointment. Did anybody know you were going to attend today?"

I had to think. "I left word with the governor's secretary and, of course, my two bodyguards told their duty officer where we were going." I gulped. "Surely you don't think *I* was their target."

"We have to consider it." Still fretting, Doc frowned. "I mean, how could the bad guys have known there would be so many civilians on that top floor?"

"Plus that Navy officer."

"Yeah... the admiral might have been another unexpected fly."

"Unless..." I squeezed my eyes shut. "Unless *she* was one of their targets."

His skeptical expression softened a bit. "Could be. She was one of two people who looked like they didn't belong there.

Her and the guy at the exit." When I held up three fingers, his eyebrows arched. "Who else?"

"You."

"Me? Why'd I look out of place?"

"This seventy-year-old jacket, plus your back to the far corner like a gunfighter, with one eye on the door."

He grinned slightly. "Always nice to know who's coming and going... especially in rooms with only one door." *A handsome smile, one it would be nice to see more of.*

"So two groups," I summarized, "the planners with the convicts holding hostages... and all those other guys who scattered when the bus doors opened."

We both watched the convicts checking residences on both sides of that street as they slowly approached Elderwood. "But we can't rule out a third party," said Doc. "Let's call them the rogues — that's what *these* guys look like."

"If they plan to stay in town for more than a few minutes," I said, "you'd think they'd be looking to change from orange jumpsuits."

A dark-complexioned man rolled up in a wheelchair and stopped right behind me, near the front windows. "So what's going on out there?" he asked. "Heather wouldn't tell us anything." He looked to be in his 90s, sturdy shoulders and upper body but frail, thin legs in loose-hanging khakis. He had a bulky zippered belly pack strapped to his lap. "I recognize Señora Temple from her visit here last year," he said while looking at Doc, "but who the hell are you?" Then he pointed to my pistol and Doc's borrowed belt rig. "And why all the firepower?"

"I took this rig off her dead bodyguard," replied my companion. "I'm Doc Holliday."

"Like Earp's buddy in Tombstone?" The old man's gray bushy eyebrows rose dramatically.

Doc groaned. "I'll tell you later, if we're both still alive." At least he didn't ignore the question as he had with me earlier. "This little downtown is under attack by two busloads of escaped convicts," he said, "and a portion of them seem to be headed this way. We're considering them rogues on some sort of mission."

"You should be in the cafeteria with the others," I suggested as diplomatically as possible. "Mister...?"

"Gregorio Rodriguez," he said proudly. "These days, everybody calls me Viejo."

"Those bad guys will probably be here as soon as they finished tossing those houses," said Doc, pointing toward one of the remaining strips of the old residential section in northern downtown. "You'd better get to safety."

"Nope," said Viejo as he set his jaw. "You aren't going to herd me into a pen to wait for someone to come in blasting. I've got a better chance here in the open where I can outrun them."

Though I struggled to keep from smiling, I realized he'd meant it sincerely.

"Besides, I can help," he added. "I know this building. Plus," he pointed to Doc's jacket, "I wore one of those Ikes when they were brand new. I was with Third Infantry Division at Messina and Salerno, and followed General Truscott to Anzio. If that's not enough, I know something about tactics."

"Tactics?" I asked.

"Sure." Then Viejo eyed Doc carefully. "What were you guys planning? Just stand here and shoot it out against convicts with bigger guns?"

"Well, I'm waiting on a call back from the governor," I said. "We believe he has an appropriate law enforcement response organized and we're just waiting to hear who they are and when they're coming."

Viejo chuckled. "Those ex-prisoners could have this whole building ransacked by the time the feds get their hostage negotiators in place."

"How do you know about the hostages?" I asked.

"I heard it with my own two eyes." Viejo smiled thinly. "Not all old folks are deaf, you know."

Doc, who had been constantly monitoring the approaching convicts, said over his shoulder, "Well, if you've got a good plan of defense, now's the time to spill it." He doubled over and backed away from the shaded windows. "We already told the receptionist to lock all the outside doors."

I made essentially his same movements, but judging from Doc's eyeballs, it probably looked a lot different for a woman in skirt and heels.

By the time I reached the counter, Viejo was already back with Doc in front of Heather's office. "Even if they're determined to get in," said the old man, "the locked double doors should hold them out for a while. Plus, we might have a few additional surprises. Including shatterproof glass in the first-floor windows."

"Shatterproof?" I asked. "Wouldn't that violate fire codes?"

"This building's renovation has lots of variance from normal construction. Rumor is the Elderwood owner saw all the vandalism and deterioration of that run-down Washington Hotel at the east edge of town and wanted *his* structure to last for a hundred years." Viejo began rolling his wheels as he barked out instructions. "Open that door, would you?"

When I did, he zipped into Heather's empty office and wheeled around to the console.

"This button," he said, pressing it with a flourish, "activates the external alarm system."

Doc gave him a puzzled expression.

"Special feature of Elderwood. Because many of our residents have substandard hearing, our alarms are about three times the volume of what you'd have in any regular apartment building."

"That might scare the crap out of a few convicts," observed Doc.

"Those are steel reinforced doors with heavy duty deadbolts, all able to be set and re-set from this panel."

"So?" I said, trying not to sound too impressed.

Doc kept his eye on the front windows.

"Except for the front door, señora, each exit has a lockable secondary inside door. On the two ends, they separate the fire escape stairwell from the main building."

Focusing again on us, Doc said, "Let's cut to the chase, Viejo."

"With these monitors, we can see if anybody breaks through the outside door and we'll know exactly where they are before they actually get inside to us."

"Monitors?" I said, surprised. "Don't remember that from the tour I had."

"They aren't usually discussed with outsiders, because people might get the wrong idea that the complex is spying on its residents."

"Are they?" I asked.

"No. The cameras only scan the outside parking lot, delivery area, and entrances, plus the hallways and public rooms."

"Punch up the cafeteria," said Doc.

With a practiced movement, Viejo displayed that room on the screen. "I fiddle with the console when Heather's not here. Gives me something to do besides TV and dominoes."

There were at least two dozen people visible in the cafeteria and — on another screen — a few more being escorted down the hallway toward it. "Does that represent everybody in the building?" I asked.

"Heather's good about headcounts," replied Viejo. "If she hasn't told you otherwise, then you can figure she's got everybody gathered... or has someone assigned to bring each of the others down."

"How do you know what we told her to do?" asked Doc.

"I read her notes," he said with a smile. "Terrible handwriting, by the way." He patted Doc's antique sleeve with its three overseas hash marks. "And a pretty good plan, too... as far as it went."

"What did we leave out?" I asked.

Viejo nodded south toward the front doors and then pointed at the other three compass directions in turn. "We have four entrance points and no way to know which one they'll try for, or if they'll try all at once."

"I'm guessing we'll know soon enough," said Doc. "So what's your plan, Viejo?"

"The cameras will reveal their approach to Fortress Elderwood. And unless they all come in the front door, I think we have them right where we want them."

CHAPTER 8

As I pondered Viejo's complacent and rather puzzling notion, the phone in my purse buzzed and I nearly wet myself. It was Governor Ampersand.

"Julia, what on earth are you doing? This daffy intern said you're in Verdeville. We've learned those buses were carrying hard-core convicted felons. Those aren't white-collar office thieves or first-offender drug busts. Now get yourself back here to the capitol!" he ordered.

"Governor, I can't leave yet. But I need to know when the cavalry is coming, who they are, and how I can communicate with them." I put him on speaker so Doc and Viejo could hear.

In the distance, to the south, we heard more automatic weapons firing.

"Was that gunfire?" asked the governor.

I was surprised he could hear it over the phone. "Yes, sir," I replied. "Most of east downtown Verdeville has been under attack, and at least half a dozen of those escaped convicts are on this very street and seem to be heading for the Elderwood Apartments."

"Oh, Lord." He could probably picture the headlines. "A massacre of seniors on my watch."

"Doesn't have to be a massacre, Governor, but we've already lost some good men. I believe Kayla told you that Todd and Denny were both killed in the annex building." My throat struggled with a ragged lump. "But I got out and I have an armed companion — a civilian. And we also have an inside strategist who's helping set up our defenses here." I touched Viejo's shoulder. "We should be able to hold out for a little while at least. Are you activating the Tennessee National Guard?"

"I have them on standby. But it'll take maybe five or six hours to recall everybody and saddle up... and probably another three or four hours to get organized and get there. These guys have jobs and families. They're not in uniform in some orderly room just sitting around ready to deploy." He cleared his throat almost silently. "Besides, they're not really trained for this kind of situation. But the feds specialize in it."

"So who *are* you activating, Governor?"

"I want you out of there, Julia, and I'm sending in our new state SWAT team to get you. They'll be there as soon as possible."

Huh?

Viejo punched up the back door's camera. "Nothing yet, señora."

"I didn't know we had a state SWAT team."

"It was a need-to-know situation, Julia. I'm sorry I didn't brief you in."

He had not briefed me about much of anything. He'd been against the new constitution's provision to have *voters* elect his lieutenant governor. Though he and my late father had been good friends for all the years Senator Temple represented our state in Washington, Ampersand seemed to regard me as little more than an annoyance in the greater governor's office complex. I'd heard him say at least once that I had no executive potential whatsoever. *Just a pretty face with nice legs.* "We can discuss those briefings later, sir. Who's the team commander?"

"Captain Lionel," Ampersand replied. "Good man. Knows his stuff."

"Excellent, I'll be looking for him." Something related occurred to me. "Governor, does anybody else know our state SWAT team is responding?"

"Glad you reminded me. They don't officially exist yet, Julia. Technically, they're still in training and are not operational. So they're not to have any contact with the federal boys once they arrive on scene."

That puzzled me, but additional distant shots from the south distracted me more. "When are the feds due to arrive?"

It sounded like the governor covered his mouthpiece and I heard his muffled voice asking someone a question. Then he returned to me. "State and county resources will be used to set up roadblocks, but those will be out pretty far. My source believes it will take at least an hour for the federal team to get into place on the downtown perimeter..."

While he continued, I tried to mentally calculate when the feds might arrive.

"... and their choppers will show up first. It's my understanding they'll assemble at the police station, uh, west of downtown, and then spread out on foot and by armored vehicle to establish a perimeter around the annex and buses. They'll zero in on the group holding the hostages, of course. It's likely they'll augment with other state and local resources to nab those convicts headed south toward the interstate, others going in different directions, and any who might be hunkered down."

"Sir, not all the convicts are still in that central area. We can't see everything from here, but we've already spotted some guys headed toward the courthouse as well as the ones looting houses and coming in this direction."

"Good to know, Julia. I'll pass that along." He stopped to mutter something to whoever was beside him. "The federal boys will isolate those pockets and put them out of commission."

I wondered if that was a euphemism for killing them, but frankly I didn't care at that point. All were convicted violent offenders; most now had weapons and were mounting attacks. If they went down, I figured they'd brought it on themselves. "Don't let them forget the organizers of this breakout... whoever they are."

"They're working on that right now." Again Ampersand whispered something, likely to a nearby aide, and then returned his attention to me. "We believe they have a few solid leads, but they're not sharing any intel with us."

Figures. "Oh, I can't remember if I told Kayla, but these guys also had explosives." I turned to Doc. "What were they?"

"Concussion grenades, as best I could tell," replied Doc.

"Whose voice is that, Julia?" asked the governor. "Have you got me on speaker?"

The second question was ignored. "Doc Holliday, sir. I used to live here, but I've been in Clarkesville for several years."

"A medical doctor could be useful."

"Not that kind of doc, Governor."

"Huh? Well, whatever you do, Holliday," said Ampersand, "stay close to Mrs. Temple 'til the SWAT team gets there."

"Will do, Governor. I'm on her."

Viejo smiled at the phrasing.

"Okay, Julia. Now, you know how those federal response teams are once they take over a situation. So our provisional state SWAT team has to disappear — with you in tow — before any of the federal task force reaches that apartment building you're in."

I'd already told him I wasn't leaving until the senior residents were safe, so I didn't bother repeating it. "We'll be watching for the SWAT guys, Governor. Be sure they know to approach from our north side."

Ampersand's phone sounded muffled again, so he was probably relaying that information to someone nearby. "Julia, until our team arrives to extract you, is there anything else you need from me?"

I thought about asking for prayers, but didn't perceive the governor to be particularly spiritual. "Are there any resources available to notify people who live in this area or happen to be downtown to stay inside and bolt their doors until this is over?"

"Who else is in that tiny downtown on a Sunday, early afternoon?"

"Don't know for certain, Governor, and it looks too late if anybody's in the courthouse... but there are a couple of banks and office buildings in this central part of Verdeville. Any way to reach whoever might be working this weekend?"

"Stand by." After a long parley with someone near him, the governor returned to me. "My emergency advisors believe if we post a general alarm, like with those civil defense tests, it could cause a panic. Greene County's alert system is not yet sophisticated enough, so we have no way of notifying selective facilities... besides not knowing which buildings might have anyone inside them, or which office phones in those structures might be near any occupants. Our unfortunate choice in this case is either to alert almost the entire county or contact no one." He paused to clear his throat silently, in that way of polished politicians. "My advisors say leave it alone and let social media and the Nashville TV stations handle it, as they will anyway. So, for whoever happens to be in downtown Verdeville at this time, I'm afraid there's nothing we can do."

Except hopefully rescue them after they become hostages. It felt like he'd given up too soon, but I had neither time nor energy to debate it. "There are also some small, older residential neighborhoods close to downtown." I gulped. "So if there's been no general alert, even more of those houses might get broken into."

"The response team will do a sweep after their main efforts. They'll be counting heads. If any convict comes up missing, they'll go house to house."

That sounded thorough, but also seemed like it could take several hours.

Outside, semi-automatic fire peppered the front door of our building. It didn't make sense for them to think they could cause real damage from what must have been a considerable distance, so maybe they were just blowing off steam. We couldn't see any holes, so that reinforced door had withstood whatever caliber weapons the felons had... probably nine millimeter. Hoped they didn't have anything heavier.

"More gunfire?" Ampersand asked anxiously.

"Yes, sir, but still from a distance, apparently," I replied. "Governor, any idea who that female admiral is?"

"No," he replied. "I asked, but as soon as I mentioned her, the feds went to dead air."

"What do you mean?"

"Not sure," said Ampersand with a heavy sigh, "but evidently she's somebody special."

Special in what way, I wondered. "I thought it was odd for her to be in full uniform... you know, unless she was here on official Navy business."

"Full uniform?" Again he whispered something to an aide.

"So they didn't give you her name?" I asked.

"No. Evidently my security classification isn't high enough."

Again, Doc whispered to me, "No admiral goes anywhere without an aide."

"Governor, I'm confused."

"As we are here at the capitol," he replied. "But unless they were trying to kidnap you, I got the impression this admiral might be the main reason they chose Verdeville for their breakout site."

CHAPTER 9

AFTER MY CALL with the governor, I just stared at the phone. Doc checked his watch and Viejo punched enough buttons to get each of the cameras' views to appear briefly on one of the three monitors.

From the front windows, we could see that all of the convicts on our street had become occupied with the modest, single family dwellings that stood between them and us. They likely didn't realize they were giving us a much-needed break.

When I sat down, finally — first time since I'd left the performance — I realized how much my feet hurt. "These heels are killing me." I nodded at Viejo. "I don't guess you have a lost and found around here with comfortable shoes in it?"

"No, señora," he replied, "but we do have some belongings of a female resident who passed on. No relative claimed her things."

"What size shoes did she wear?"

He smiled. "Mrs. Pollard was only a tiny woman... small features." He held his hands about six inches apart. "Her feet maybe this big."

"Great," I said, with no attempt to restrain my sarcasm. "That's at least two sizes too small." When I started to cross my legs, I noticed thin streams of blood running down my shins.

Both men were also staring.

"Skinned my knees on the pavement," I said with a shrug.

"There's an infirmary directly above us," said Viejo, pointing to a floor plan of the main level. The map indicated *Nurse Station.*

As Doc scrambled up the main stairs, I leaned my head back and closed my eyes. But before I could actually doze off, he was back with a handful of first aid supplies. It looked like gauze and hydrogen peroxide... and maybe a few Band-Aids. I reached for the supplies. "Thanks."

"No, you go ahead and rest your eyes. I'll treat your wounds."

"So you *are* a medic?"

Viejo chuckled but stayed out of our conversation.

"I've been lots of things," said Doc cryptically.

And I still had no idea what he meant. "Thank you, Doc," I said, "but I really can do this myself."

He gave me a stern look as he knelt beside my chair. "You're a public servant and you're elected to do the will of the populace. Consider me a representative of that constituency and this is what I want you to do. Just sit there and relax and let me handle this." Then he peered closely. "No telling how bad these are and you don't want them to scar."

If I'd had more strength, a clearer head, and less stress knotting my belly, perhaps I would've realized I had no business letting a total stranger touch my legs. But, after all, I reasoned, he did say we'd met before...

So I leaned my head back and closed my eyes. I felt Doc's strong hand holding each calf as he tenderly dabbed the hydrogen peroxide over the scraped areas and swabbed away the rivulets that tickled as they ran down my legs. He'd also brought some paper towels, which he used to dry the remainder.

For those moments, as I felt warm and relaxed, the sensation of a man's hands on my legs reminded me of nights long ago. But new gunfire, outside to the south — fainter, and therefore likely more distant. Doc and Viejo briefly discussed whether it was rifles or pistols. I couldn't really tell which was which, though I certainly detected a difference in the sharpness of the report. Whatever firearms were blazing far outside, they roused me back to the harsh reality of our present situation. I bolted upright and surveyed his first aid work. "Thank you, Doc. Looks very nice."

"Yes, they do."

"Beg your pardon?"

"Your legs. I thought I'd already mentioned that."

I blushed like a schoolgirl. "Uh, I'm gratified at your compliments — then and now — but I must say that a woman with decent legs can also be a perfect bitch. So you can't judge a whole person by the shape of what she walks upon."

Viejo, off to one end of the control room, suddenly wheeled past us and exited through the blocked-open door. Either he figured we needed some privacy or he was having difficulty restraining his amusement at our conversation.

"Oh, I wasn't judging," continued Doc. "The rest of you, physically, I mean, was — and I'd say, still is — lovely indeed. But even as a horny teenager, I was able to look past beauty and see substance."

Glad he'd found some. "Anything in particular?"

"Yeah. You could've blown us off. A small class from a hick town. The boss is gone and you're just working there. The entire exchange might've lasted about two minutes and we could've been brushed out of your hair."

"Then I'm glad I didn't brush you off."

"More than that. You cared — or convinced me that you cared. And it was easy to see how proud you were of your father's service to our state and our nation. It made me feel proud of him and I'd never even seen him in person."

"Dad always said it was an honor to serve... and he meant it. Wasn't always easy, and he made lots of political enemies, but he consistently did what he thought was best for Tennessee folks and Americans in general." I had the feeling Doc still wasn't telling me everything about that earlier encounter. "Well, anyway, thanks for explaining, uh, further... and, you know..."

"You're too modest, I suppose, to realize the effect you have on people."

My face warmed again. "Not sure what you mean."

"It was intoxicating to be that close to someone so beautiful, so full of life, so engrossed and excited by what she was doing and who she represented. It was almost like touching the wires of a live circuit."

My mind sputtered with how to reply. Fortunately, a few additional rifle and pistol shots in the distance refocused both of us.

Viejo wheeled back through the open doorway with concern in his dark eyes. "Señora, if we're going to play Alamo," he said, "we'd better get these folks organized."

"You want me to go?" asked Doc.

Before I could reply, Heather — a distressed expression contorting her face — reappeared suddenly in the large open window to her own office. "Ma'am, the residents are getting restless in the cafeteria. Some think we ought to head for the basement where we sit out tornadoes. Can you come say a word or give them some kind of update?"

"Yes, I'm coming, but don't let anybody go downstairs. This particular tornado we're facing is one where we need to be able to exit outdoors in a hurry if things go crazy inside. So we all stay together and it's on this main floor."

"Very well, but please hurry. They need to see somebody official."

I touched Doc's muscled forearm.

"Okay, I'll stay here and watch the front door," he said. "You go calm the troops."

"Thanks." As I exited, I faced Viejo with an unspoken question.

"I'll keep monitoring these screens," he said. "I have the east and west doors on constantly and I'm using the third screen to check all the other cameras."

"Come get me if anything changes," I said and then trotted after Heather toward the cafeteria.

As I entered, I saw scattered snacks at nearly every table — besides a few sandwiches, there were candy wrappers and ice cream sticks. *Maybe a crisis boosts their appetites.* A few residents near the door started to make a fuss, as though I were a celebrity. During the entire 24 months since the election, I'd never felt like one — it always seemed I was the token woman, never taken seriously. But especially not a celebrity now... with skinned knees, rumpled skirt, and my hair probably going nineteen different directions.

"Pleased to meet you, ma'am," said one lady in a motorized scooter. "Even though I voted for your competitor."

I nodded as I tried to grasp the scope of our problem: keeping these 27 seniors from harm and protecting their facility and two on-site staff. Truly wished the governor had allowed me in the state's upper level security briefings. Wished I'd been given some actual training on handling real crises. Wished I didn't feel like an ornament with no executive potential. Wished I'd worn my sneakers instead of those heels.

"Thank you for assembling here so quickly and quietly," I said, loudly enough for even the nearly deaf to hear. Then I turned to Heather. "Is this everybody in the facility?"

"Yes, except for Viejo in the control room and our janitor in the basement."

"Can you page the janitor from your office?"

She nodded.

"Get the janitor moving this direction while I finish the briefing here."

As Heather scurried away, I overheard a very deaf old woman in the corner loudly comment about my divorce, apparently indignant that I'd re-taken my maiden name, and wondering to her tablemate why I couldn't keep a man. Actually, I didn't *want* Arnold Bane hanging around, especially after I saw how the thought of my campaign filled him with jealous dread… or something. He'd behaved just as a spoiled narcissist could be expected to.

CHAPTER 10

"WE DON'T HAVE a lot of time, folks," I said to the cafeteria assembly, "so I'll keep this short." I related what had happened at the annex, what little we knew about the reasons for the breakout, and the few things we'd surmised. The residents already seemed to understand the rapidly scattering escapees would be rounded up in a perimeter cinch by some mix of law enforcement. Then I explained the state SWAT team was heading our way, while the federal response force was assembling to deal with the core group of hostage-holders.

Amid murmurs and very loud whispers, one woman appeared to faint. Someone at her table immediately began tending her, so I continued. "The small group of convicts who appear likely interested in our building have already fired some shots this direction, but have not made actual contact with us. However, I'm told this facility was constructed to withstand anything less than a Sherman tank, so we should be safe until the professionals arrive to reinforce us."

"Are we going to be evacuated?" asked an old man sitting near his fragile-looking, outdated walker.

"It's my hope and belief that we can keep everyone secure and inside," I answered.

One woman slowly stood, holding her tripod cane tightly. "My name's Tureen. Some of us can still get around. What can we do to help?"

Not sure why hearing her offer caused a catch in my throat, but I had to lower my face to keep them from seeing the sudden moisture in my eyes.

In a thin, reedy voice, another woman — leaning on a newer, sturdier walker than the man had — also volunteered. "After 88 years, I can spot a woodpecker sweeping its nest in the next county," she said modestly. "I'm Sylvie and I'll be your, um, *watchguard*."

"Thank you, ma'am," I replied to Sylvie. "Thank you both. Yes, I'm sure we'll need some assistance, but mainly with keeping things calm in here." I looked to see if Heather had returned, but she hadn't. "Is there a specific name for this space?"

"We just call it the cafeteria," said Tureen, "but when the tables are moved, it doubles as a meeting room and we even have little concerts here."

I felt the need to give it a more glamorous name like the safe room or, as Viejo had mentioned, the Alamo — but suddenly both seemed too trite. Plus, we were running out of time and didn't need any extra confusion. "Cafeteria is good," I said. "And we may need those tables to be folded and stacked up against the windows. Is there anyone besides the janitor who could help with that?"

A gangly man who looked mobile and reasonably fit stood and cleared his throat. "I'm... not... the... fastest... color... in... the... box... but... I... can... lift... and... tote." With him, a five-second speech lasted a full minute.

"Fine," I said. "When the janitor comes in, please help him with those tables."

"Yes... ma'am..." he drawled. "I'm... Glover."

I just nodded because we needed to move on. "The rest of you, please huddle your chairs near the kitchen area and be ready to duck into the kitchen itself if any of those criminals actually gain entry. With all the appliances in there, it should be the safest place from stray bullets." As I said all that, I realized my details might have added more fear than explanation, but I needed them to cooperate quickly and completely, so I didn't hold anything back. "Tureen and Sylvie, come with me. The rest of you, please do what you can safely to help shift these chairs."

As I hurried from the Alamo cafeteria, I encountered Heather and the janitor on their way in. I gave them the quick version of my plan and then continued on to the main lobby where Doc waited with Viejo. The two helpful ladies were still en route behind me.

"I've got a volunteer spotter named Sylvie," I said to Viejo. "What's the best vantage point for her, where she won't be in harm's way?"

Viejo considered the situation. "Actual best spot is on the floor above. A little hallway comes out over this front door."

"But that would have her separate from everyone and communication could become dicey, even if she has a cell phone," I concluded. "Where else?"

Doc clutched my elbow. "Just place her to the far side of the front door. With that shatterproof glass, she won't be in any danger from bullets and they'll likely be aiming at the doors anyway."

Viejo nodded. "I can notch off the end of one of those blinds and Sylvie will be able to see all the way to the interstate." More hyperbole.

"Okay, Viejo, take care of that," I said. "And help Sylvie get situated. Here she comes now."

He rolled that direction and steered Sylvie and her walker toward the window about twenty feet to the right side of the front main door.

Tureen stopped in front of me and planted her tripod cane with emphasis. "Where do you need me?"

"Right now, monitor those screens and report anything you see. When Viejo gets back, I may need you to be my liaison with the cafeteria group."

"The only reason I use this cane is because of my new hip," she said, pointing both to the tripod and her left hip. "Titanium. I've been through rehab and they say I'm doing fine."

"Fine enough to be my runner if I need one?" I asked.

"Runner might be stretching it, but I can amble pretty good."

I smiled and touched her shoulder. "Ambling should be fine. The main thing is for us to stay in contact with the cafeteria group and be sure they know what we know."

"This control board has a P.A. system we can use for that," said Tureen, pointing vaguely toward the console. "Ought to cut down on the ambling up and down the hall."

"Good point. Do you know how to use it?"

"I've seen it in operation and can probably figure it out," she answered.

"Okay. Anyway, Viejo should be back here shortly. He's the anchor for this console. Ask him for the quick briefing in case I need to pull him away for something else."

"Roger," said Tureen, the word so incongruous from her elderly lips that I had to smile.

"Wilco," I replied, trying to look serious.

"Are you going to be darting back and forth?" asked Doc as I exited the control room, which faced the front doors and spacious lobby.

"Why?"

"Well, I wondered what you had in mind for me." His expression suggested he'd said it wrong. "I mean, whether you want me in one particular place or just as a rover."

"What's your suggestion, Doc?"

He looked into my eyes with worry on his face. "I was going to suggest we stay together, because the governor said I'm responsible for you until the SWAT team arrives..."

Though I didn't see it that way, I didn't interrupt him.

"...but since we're the only ones with guns, I guess it's better if we split up."

In a paperback novel, this could have been a tender moment with longing glances and maybe a tentative kiss, but in real life, we were talking about firepower and how to defend 27 seniors from a mob of hostile, violent felons. "I think we'll both be zipping back and forth," I replied, quite *un*romantically. "But let's be certain we keep each other apprised of what we're doing. Don't want any friendly fire accidents."

As Doc nodded acknowledgement, Viejo rolled back over to us, still in front of the control room.

"I'm antsy about these exterior doors," I said. "Can you two go check them again?"

"We can do that from here, señora. Remember?" said Viejo, rolling through the open doorway and positioning himself behind the console.

With Tureen and Doc also looking on, Viejo pointed to a row of lights and explained them. "This is all four outside doors on the first floor." All burned red. "They're fire doors, so they can be opened from the inside with an emergency press bar, but from the outside, they're like a vault."

"What about those inside doors you mentioned earlier?" I pointed vaguely to the east and west.

"Not quite as heavy as the outside doors, plus the inside ones have a small reinforced window," explained Viejo. "But they're also locked and unlocked from this panel."

"And also have the breaker bar for emergency exit?" I asked.

He nodded.

"Those lights change color when any of those doors open?" asked Doc.

Viejo nodded. "If the door's unlocked or opened, the light burns green."

"Okay," I said. "Keep them all red. If you see a green light, call me." I remembered the janitor's domain. "How many doors to the basement?"

"One on each end, east and west, at the very bottom of the enclosed fire escape," Viejo said, "and the inside stairway behind this office. Plus the elevator, of course."

"Keep the elevator on the first floor lobby with the doors open," I said. "Can you work that from the console, or do you have to set something inside the elevator?"

"Either way," he replied, "but there's an override button here." Viejo pointed so all of us could see, then he punched it, an amber light glowing immediately. In a moment the elevator car, presumably already on the first floor, opened its door and dinged loudly.

Doc placed his hand on Viejo's sturdy shoulder. "Everything I've seen so far runs on electric power. What happens if the bad guys cut the power to this place?"

My heart stopped. I pictured the emergency doors opening wide and seniors tumbling outside as the convicts hacked them to pieces...

"No problemo," said Viejo. "There's an auxiliary generator system in the basement that's powerful enough to run a small hospital."

Doc whistled softly. "This place is perfect."

Just as my heart was about to stop pounding, Sylvie's reedy voice called us to the bank of front windows. After Doc and I raced over, we peered between the blinds at the two orange jumpsuits she'd spotted just over a block away. No sign of the other four from that northernmost group. "Are those the guys you're worried about?"

"Yeah," said Doc. "Them and about forty others."

Everybody was exaggerating — surely at least thirty of the convicts had already scattered to the four winds. We didn't know how many had remained with the presumed hostages, but we were figuring ten or fewer. But it still made absolutely no sense for this small gaggle to be heading in our direction.

"Did you see where the other four went?" Doc asked Sylvie.

"Two went into one house," she said, pointing to a short row of residences left over from earlier days when downtown had been ringed by modest homes, "and two more went into the place next door."

"Any sign of the residents or what the convicts are doing?" I asked.

"I saw a few people running from their back doors," said Sylvie, "so hopefully that's all the residents. But I think some of them stole liquor, because one of the orange men is sitting on the porch drinking."

Even squinting, I could barely see that far.

"That could be good for us," said Doc. "The drunker they get, the easier it'll be to neutralize them."

"But what if they're mean drunks?" I asked, having seen a few biker movies in my younger days. "Wonder why these guys are still hanging around downtown Verdeville... instead of disappearing into the countryside?"

"That's been bothering me, too," said Doc. "My guess is they have some business here — or think they do."

That iced over my innards. "What kind of business?"

"Um, Mizz Temple," interrupted Sylvie, tugging at my gray wool-blend sleeve with an arthritic hand. "I think we've got another situation."

CHAPTER 11

"WHAT? WHERE?" I hunkered over sufficiently to duplicate the visibly stooped Sylvie's line of sight. "Oh, crap!"

"What's the problem now?" asked Doc as he grabbed my shoulders and moved me aside so he could see.

In the office building cattycorner from us — actually to the west across one alley and to the south across another alley — a woman stood in an open third-floor window waving a sign. Even my eyeballs could clearly make out a giant question mark on the piece of poster board she was sweeping back and forth.

"Doc, get some butcher paper or something and show her the main number to that console. We need her to call so we can tell her to lock her doors and stay put."

Viejo had heard my instructions and said, "No posters and no butcher paper, but we can print one number on each page and hold up seven pages."

"Do it," I said, sounding a lot more decisive than I felt. What I wanted to do was hug my knees inside a blanket fort and sip hot cocoa laced with bourbon. *Or some kind of booze.*

Viejo, Tureen, and Doc set about to produce Elderwood's phone number in large enough letters that the third-floor woman in a building some 150 feet away could see them. In short order, Doc brought over those seven pages and the other two helpers followed close behind.

I raised the blinds of that bank of windows about three feet from the bottom sill. With each of them holding two signs, Sylvie bracing the seventh page, and me biting my nails, we had the main Elderwood number on display.

The distant woman seemingly saw our signs, but continued to wave her question mark frantically.

It took Viejo to figure out we had the three-digit prefix in reverse order. He made the adjustments and everyone held their breath. The woman disappeared from her window and in about twenty seconds, the control room's phone rang.

Even though we'd told her to call, the phone's blaring noise still made me jump twelve feet in the air. I probably wasn't actually faster than Doc, but the adrenaline seemed to propel me first to the phone.

"Elderwood. Who's this?"

"Your sign, my sign, third-floor window." She was in tears. "Gunshots. What's going on?"

"Calm down," I said. "What's your name?"

"Britney. What's happening?"

"Britney, some convicts have escaped from two prison buses." I proceeded to give her the complete but condensed briefing as my eyes scanned the monitors. No activity at the east and west doors, and all the cafeteria people had dutifully clustered their chairs near the entrance to the kitchen. At the front windows, since no one had thought to bring her a chair, Sylvie stretched from her walker and lowered the blinds back to their fully down positions.

"Who are *you*?" Britney asked.

I gave her my name and title, but there was no point in trying to explain why I was there. "Are you alone in your building?" I put her on speaker.

"As far as I know, yeah. I'm not even supposed to be here, because we aren't allowed in the building on Sundays. But I didn't get through with my work yesterday." She sobbed. "So nobody knows I'm here."

"Settle down, Britney," I said, though actually I felt like crying along with her. "Are your building doors locked?"

"Yeah. I got in with my key code."

"Okay, then you just sit tight. These guys shouldn't have any interest in your building anyhow."

"But I've heard gunfire and explosions. I'm worried."

I told her about the SWAT team en route. "When they get here, I'll tell them where you are and they can come for you, too."

"Are you really the lieutenant governor?"

"Yes."

"Mrs. Temple, I don't want to be alone."

Doc motioned to me. Something he didn't want Britney to hear.

"Look, I have to put you on hold for a second. But I'm coming right back, okay?"

"Okay, but hurry."

Button, tapped. "What?" I asked Doc.

"If she can get to her back door, the one closest to our west entrance, I can rush over there and escort her back in three shakes."

"What about those guys in orange?"

"They're busy with that row of houses for the moment. If we move fast, we can get this woman over here and the bad guys won't see a thing."

"But what if they do?"

Viejo spoke up. "We could mount a distraction at the east entrance."

"What kind?"

"Oh, something subtle. You step outside the door, señora, and toss some firecrackers in the air."

"Yeah," said Doc. "The bad guys duck down and look to the northeast, while me and the girl are hustling in at the other end."

"I don't exactly carry fireworks in my purse," I replied. "Could I just shoot this pistol?"

"Danger of hitting somebody in the distance," said Viejo.

Doc added two cents: "Plus, we don't really want them to know we have any guns here."

I groaned. "So where do I get firecrackers?"

"Wally the janitor had some on his desk downstairs," suggested Viejo. "Left over from July Fourth. And if those are gone, I still have some from Cinco de Mayo."

Doc was already heading down the inside stairs.

"Okay... could work." I closed my eyes and pictured it. "Viejo, it'll mean you operating two sets of exit door locks. Split-second timing."

"No problemo. I'll know by the monitors the exact second I need to unlock them."

I punched the hold button and got back on the line with Britney — still on speaker. "Okay, we've worked out a plan, but you'll have to move fast. Can you see our west-end door from where you are?"

"Which side is west?"

"Viejo, tell her what the door looks like."

"West side has two planters with flowers, lady. Do you see it?"

"Flowers. Yeah."

"Okay, Britney," I said, "are you on your cell phone?"

"Uh, no. Actually this is the office line. I couldn't find my cell."

"Is it in your purse?"

"Hold on and I'll check." It took a few seconds. "Found it. Had it in my pocket."

"Okay, hang up and call us back from your cell phone. Keep us connected while you take the stairs down to the exit door nearest our west end."

Her nerves were too tight to be polite. She simply clicked off the connection. Doc reappeared with an opened pack of ordinary, cheap firecrackers. As we waited for the main Elderwood phone to ring again, I checked with our guard on the walker at the front windows. Despite the sharpness of our lookout's eyes, her body posture looked old and exhausted — I'd have to get her a chair soon. "Any updates, Sylvie?"

"Three orange jumpsuits from that row of houses have joined the two out on the street. The one on the porch hasn't moved. He's still drinking." Sylvie turned to face us. "From the look of things, I'm guessing he's their leader. You know, body language."

So the northernmost group remained a full block away. Good. But it still made no sense for them to be lingering downtown.

Ring! Despite expecting the call, we all jumped. Britney, this time on her cell phone. She narrated her movements through the building as she took the stairs to the second floor and then the first. "Okay, I'm on the main level."

"Are you at an exit?" I asked.

"Yeah, looking though the door's little window."

"Don't open that door yet," I said. "Can you see our west entrance?"

"Yeah, I can still see your building, but this door is way further down my building."

"Terrific," I said, with disgust. "Hold on, Britney. Sylvie, can you see their rear door from here?"

"Not from here, no."

"What's immediately outside your door, Britney?"

"Um, a big ugly tree that looks like it's dead. They've been talking about chopping it down for six months."

"Sylvie, can you see a large dead tree?"

Her thin voice called back, "Yes, just a bit past mid-point of the building, but that door must be behind a partial brick wall or something."

"I think they keep their dumpster back there," added Viejo.

"All right, Britney. Stay on the line. Do not hang up. We're sending over Doc Holliday—"

"I don't need a doctor, I need a cop or a soldier!"

"Never mind, Britney. *Mister* Holliday will sprint past the dumpster enclosure and large tree, directly to your door." I took a deep breath. "Is that the exact door where you are?"

"Yeah. Dumpster, tree. That's me."

"Okay, when I see Doc in position at the end of this hall, I'll signal Viejo to unlock both these doors and that signals you to start counting to thirty. When you get to thirty, open the door, unless you see him first."

"What does he look like?"

"Has on a state trooper's belt rig, but in civilian clothes. He's tall and handsome... and, by the time you see him, sweaty."

Doc shrugged off his Ike jacket and handed it to Viejo. "Hold this for me, will you?"

"Gladly, señor." He embraced it like a long-lost friend.

Doc handed me the firecrackers and a lighter. "Found this on the desk downstairs. Okay, I'm off." He trotted down the hallway, paused by the inside exit door, and waved like I might not see him again.

Someone from my past whom I didn't even remember was departing. Suddenly my heart clenched. In the short time we'd been together — again — we'd hardly had a chance to do anything but run and plan, but I'd begun to feel a closeness with him. And hopefully there'd be time to see if he felt it also. But at the moment, we had to rescue a damsel — presumably a registered voter.

I motioned to Viejo, who punched the buttons to unlock both that inside and outside door. Both panel lights immediately turned green. I signaled Doc and he disappeared at the end of that long hallway. "Okay, Britney, he's on his way. Count to thirty and keep your eyes in that window." To Viejo, I gave the cutthroat sign, meaning *lock those doors*. When he punched the buttons, those lights again burned red.

My guts turned icy. "Sylvie, let me know when you see them heading back our way."

"I've got my eyes peeled," she replied in her reedy voice.

"I'll keep watch on the monitor, señora," said Viejo, "so we'll know when they are close."

Tureen had abandoned her tripod cane, evidently deciding she could move better without it. I grabbed her elbow and told her to stand where I'd been and watch Sylvie, Viejo, and the end of the west hallway for any development. "I'm heading down to that east exit and try to distract those orange guys if they focus on our building." Then, to Viejo, I said, "When Tureen sees that I've reached the end of the hall, unlock both those doors and keep them clear 'til I jump back inside."

"Wait," he said urgently. "You don't need to stick your head outside after all. I'd forgotten you can see that direction through the corner room." He checked an emergency evacuation floor plan posted near the console. "Room 1-15." In case I needed it, he even pointed that direction. "Just unlock that window and toss out the firecrackers."

Good idea. *Why didn't I think of that?* The stress was getting to me. No wonder people said I had no executive potential. I was about to stick my head out the door to check for bad guys where there was a perfectly good window in a corner room that would give me an excellent view. "Right. Good thinking. Is that room locked?"

"Hardly any of the individual rooms are ever locked unless that resident is away for a hospital stay or something."

"Or out visiting for the day?" I asked.

"Oh, yeah. Hang on." He quickly checked a resident sign-in-sign-out file on the console's computer screen. "No sweat, 1-15 belongs to Glover and he's here. So his door won't be locked."

I realized I had wasted at least half of the time Britney was supposedly counting down. And I'd had Britney on speaker phone the whole time. "Are you still there, Britney?"

"Yeah. What's all that about doors and windows?"

"Never mind. Do you see our man yet?"

"Uh, not yet. Oh, wait. Yeah! Just coming around the corner."

He'd made good time.

"You want me to let him in?"

"Not *in*, Britney. He's your escort back to our building. Just open the door, meet him, and take off."

"Can I hang up now?"

"Yes! Scram!" I shouted as I ran panting down the east hallway. I reached Room 1-15, barged in, and zoomed to the corner window. Didn't see any progress from the orange jumpsuits, except that the man who'd been drinking on the porch was now rejoining the other five convicts standing on the corner of Pierce and Ash.

I'd screwed up the delicate timing of our operation and my planned distraction was already too late. My guts froze again. One of the others had been looking vaguely northwest and obviously saw Britney and Doc zipping back toward Elderwood. With the distance and the closed window, I couldn't actually discern what he said, but I definitely heard him shout. It sounded like, "Hey, look! A woman!" And everyone in orange turned and stared.

CHAPTER 12

ICE FORMED AGAIN in my belly at the realization that I'd screwed up the diversion and the bad guys had spotted Doc and Britney. Small wonder nobody thought I had any executive potential. Still clutching the fireworks and lighter, I fled Room 1-15 and sprinted back up the east hallway, my shoulder bag flapping against my hip with every step. "Viejo, open those doors and get ready to lock 'em back down quick."

"Friendlies approaching our building," called out Sylvie in her thin voice. Then she added, "Holliday and the girl," in case we needed the clarification.

"On the monitor," said Viejo as he clicked both door lock buttons.

Sailing right by the control room and into the west corridor, I reached the inside door just a moment after Doc stepped through it with a terrified Britney in tow. Seeing his strong arm around her trembling shoulders made me strangely jealous, but I was too overwrought to think about it. "Are y'all okay?"

He nodded and passed Britney off to me for more comfort than he seemed able or willing to provide. She felt strange in my stiff arms and I realized I, too, lacked the ability to comfort her. Sobbing, Britney tried to vocalize her questions. Thankfully, Tureen had followed me down the hall and embraced the frightened girl, who then collapsed into her elderly, comforting embrace.

"They're in. Lock the doors," I yelled, though it was hardly necessary since Viejo was closely monitoring every movement. The electronic lock clacked loudly in the near inside door after Viejo punched the console buttons.

"What happened to our distraction?" asked Doc, panting. "Didn't hear your fireworks."

"My fault. *I* got distracted." As the four of us tried to hurry along the long west hallway, I told Doc I was certain the bad guys had seen them running this way.

"Yeah, I heard somebody shouting and saw some of them pointing. They spotted us, all right."

"Does that change anything in our strategy?" I asked.

"Seeing the girl probably gave them more incentive to get inside this building sooner, rather than later," he replied, apparently not aware of how terrifying that would sound to Britney, "since they're still hanging around downtown instead of scattering. So it's probably tweaked their timetable, but not their destination. I'm just about positive they'd already decided on tackling this retirement home... for the reasons we've already discussed and possibly some others we don't know about yet."

"And now they have a brand new reason to want inside," I added, before realizing that would also frighten Britney.

"My baby's at my mom's," said Britney, her voice quavering as she clutched at Tureen. "I need to let them know I'm all right."

I asked Tureen to take the frightened young woman to the cafeteria. "Once she gets settled, give her a chance to make that call."

Tureen shifted her weight to her natural hip. "You want me to stay there or come back here?"

"After you get her situated, I need you back here," I said.

They took off, Tureen using her exaggerated loping stride to accommodate that new hip she was still getting used to.

Viejo held up the Ike jacket. "You want this back now, Doc?"

Mopping the sweat from his face, Doc replied, "Too hot at the moment. You mind hanging on to it for me?"

"Gladly," he said, smiling. "It feels like an old buddy." He draped it over the rear handles of his wheelchair but rested the long, heavy sleeves on his shoulders.

My phone vibrated and I jumped. The governor again. No chit-chat this time... straight to business, and I put him on speaker. "The feds are handling everything," said Ampersand.

"Sir, how long will it take them to get here and stabilize things?"

"Fact is, we don't know. My advisors are still crossing their fingers for that first estimate." He paused as if checking something on his end.

"Which was?"

"Their advance team should be arriving before three o'clock."

That would be in an hour or so. "What about our SWAT guys?"

"Aren't they on site yet?"

"No, Governor. Haven't seen..."

He cut me off, barking orders to the people near him. "Get ahold of Captain Lionel and find out what's keeping them."

"Governor, while we're waiting on that info, let me update you on something here. We came across a woman in the offices next door. She believes she was alone in the building. We now have her here with us, safely, but in that transition, the small group of convicts on our street and possibly coming our way evidently spotted her."

"Okay. Good. Glad she's safe." He seemed not to understand the significance of them noticing her. "Hope nobody else is working in that little burg's downtown."

"Probably not, sir, but we've also seen some forced entries to a few houses along Pierce Avenue. As best we can tell, the residents apparently fled on foot. Hopefully on their way to safety."

"What we should've done," muttered Doc.

Apparently the governor didn't hear him. "Any damages?"

"Nothing visible from here, but we're assuming they rifled through those houses looking for valuables and maybe a change of clothes. Only thing we've actually seen them with was some stolen booze."

"We're anticipating property damage," he said. "But hopefully no fires... because in a hostage situation like this, the fire crews aren't usually allowed in."

Yeah, just let the structures burn down. "Any word on those survivors from the annex?"

"We're not exactly in the loop with these federal response people, but as far as we know there's been no official contact yet from the escapees."

"So no idea how many hostages, or their condition?" I asked.

"All we know about hostages came from your report, Julia."

"Probably the prison transport guards and almost certainly the Navy officer," I said. "Any I.D. yet on that admiral?"

"Just a high-value target," replied Ampersand. "They always try to keep alive someone valuable to them."

"Somebody get over here," Sylvie's reedy voice called out. "The Orange Men are moving again."

"Governor, I've got to go. Let me know what you find out about the ETA on our SWAT team."

"Will do, Julia. And when they do get to you, you're coming out with them."

My feeble great aunt had died in a New Orleans nursing home during Hurricane Katrina in 2005. At some facilities, a few very sick patients had been mercy-killed after their meds ran out and power lost to their machines. *I'm not leaving these old folks alone.* "I'm sorry, Governor, but I'm staying."

He'd just begun to sputter when I clicked off the phone and scampered toward Sylvie, still leaning on her walker. I kept thinking somebody would have brought her a chair by now... but I was among those who hadn't. "What is it?" I asked.

Doc, already there, was peering in all possible directions. "Back up," he said in a loud hiss. "Clear the windows. They're here!"

We each clutched one of Sylvie's elbows so she wouldn't topple. Tureen, who'd just returned from the cafeteria, grabbed her friend's walker as we swiftly cleared that space and headed back toward the control room, which faced the front's double doors.

"You sure that door's solid?" I asked Viejo.

"Fort Knox keeps extra gold here," he replied with an earnest expression.

Doc started pulling at people. "Well, just in case, everybody hunker down behind this counter."

When we did, only our five faces appeared above the counter. I started to pull Trooper Todd's gun from my purse, but Doc touched my wrist. *Not yet.*

We heard one of the convicts try the front door. When he found it locked, he began banging on it... then yelling and kicking. After a short silence, he fired a few shots and added vile curses. The cleanest version was, "Let us in or we'll blow this place up."

As Doc put his finger to his lips and eyeballed each of us, we all held our breath.

"There's some payback coming to old lady Pollard," screeched the one making all the racket who we perceived as their leader, "and I plan to deliver it in person."

No guesses about the motives of the other five convicts, but finally we understood *his* reason for remaining in downtown Verdeville.

CHAPTER 13

AFTER THAT INITIAL contact from the convicts, things were strangely quiet out front. Too quiet. "Viejo, are there any cameras that show outside the front doors?"

He nodded as he punched a few buttons and switched the third screen to front camera. That left east and west exits on their own screens, but a temporary blackout on the rear exit.

"Don't see anyone out front," I said. "Can you redirect those cameras at all?"

Viejo shook his head as his brown fingers hovered over the buttons and dials. "No, they're all fixed."

I tapped the old man's sturdy shoulder. "What was that about payback for Mizz What's-her-name?"

"He called out Mrs. Pollard," replied Viejo slowly. "She's the resident who died recently. We talked about her shoes. Remember?"

"Why would an escaped convict be interested in Mrs. Pollard?" I asked.

"He said payback," interjected Doc, "so the old lady must've had something to do with him being arrested."

"The trial!" exclaimed Tureen, shifting back off her titanium hip. "Neva Pollard was taken to the Verdeville courthouse — back in January, I think — to testify in a Nashville trial."

"I remember that," added Sylvie, trying to squeeze her walker closer to the conversation. "Some sort of video hookup that the Nashville judge allowed because she was too frail to travel."

"Well, whatever she testified about is evidently in that guy's craw," said Doc.

That's a wrinkle we could do without.

"I know," said Tureen. "Just tell them poor Neva Pollard has already passed."

There was a moment of silence as we considered that logical suggestion.

Viejo spoke first. "They wouldn't believe it. Besides, once you get revenge on your mind, you're more focused on the payback than on who gets paid."

All the payback talk had me confused. What did the leader of those dangerous armed convicts have in mind? "We need to know where those guys went to."

Doc rose from his crouch but ducked behind the side column of the large control room window area. "I'll go." He unholstered Trooper Denny's pistol and eased back the slide to be sure a round was chambered. Evidently habit, since he'd checked it before. Then he flipped off the safety. "Be right back." That final consonant still hung in the control room as he dashed across the lobby space to the front bank of windows. His back to the front wall, he held the pistol up, his forefinger resting against the trigger guard, and snuck a peek through the aperture in the blinds which Sylvie had been using for her eagle-eyed scouting.

Apparently seeing nothing, he hunkered over and dashed to the far side of the opposite bank of windows. With a deep breath and his back against that wall, he repeated the maneuver, but this time with no aperture, so he had to raise a blind slightly.

Rat-tat-tat-tat-tat! Automatic weapon fire against that bank of windows. Since the initial attack in the annex, all we'd heard was semi-auto.

Having dived to the floor, Doc then combat-crawled toward the west hallway, where he stood again — appearing a little pale — and looked in our direction. His pistol back on safety and holstered, he used hand signals to indicate four of the bad guys were standing back a bit from the front doors. Not clear how far back.

I held up two fingers to ask about the other two we'd seen earlier.

Doc shook his head and dashed down the west hallway.

When I started to race down the east corridor to check, Viejo stopped me and pointed at the screens. "Nothing on the cameras."

"Both ends?" I asked.

He punched some buttons. "Not at the back door either."

"Wonder where they went."

By then Doc had come racing back and skidded to a stop at the entrance to the control room. "Thought I heard something down at that end, but I didn't see anything from Room 1-06. Did you notice that last burst was full auto?"

I nodded and swallowed hard. "Wonder where they got machine guns?"

"I don't think the guards carried them," said Doc. "If not, then the criminals who planned this whole thing must've brought the automatic weapons."

"Did you see anything at that end?" I asked.

"No sign of the other two convicts."

"What about the four out front?" I pointed that direction.

"They're just cooling their heels out at that fountain thing," Doc replied.

"How far away is the fountain, Viejo?"

Viejo squinted his dark brown eyes to calculate. "About half a football field, señora."

"Okay, that missing pair really bothers me." I looked at a large framed photo, presumably taken from a helicopter or a drone, of the Elderwood complex, situated as it was in the middle of two square blocks, which interrupted and re-routed the traffic on Pierce Avenue. The structure faced south, with a straight shot down Pierce all the way to Main Street. To each side were alleys connecting to Fillmore and Buchanan; Hickory bordered the north side of those two square blocks, while Ash bordered the south.

The photo showed the front with several officials lined up — probably including me if that was the grand opening about fifteen months ago. "Are the windows on the second floor as heavy duty as these down here?" None of the small arms fire had yet broken any lower-level glass.

Viejo's eyes grew wide. "No, those upstairs are just ordinary glass."

Doc's pained expression looked like he was about to lay an egg. "Anything outside that somebody could climb?"

As Viejo considered his reply, I scanned the photo again. On the west end, only the two beds of flowers. But the east side door was straddled by two tall trees. "Could somebody climb those and get in a window?"

Doc started to sprint down that corridor, but I grabbed at his arm. Missed the arm, but connected with his muscled midsection. "Wait."

Viejo pointed to the framed floor plan. "There is a window at the end, but it's only to the emergency stairwell, which is almost completely separate from the main building. Like I told you before, those doors — if they're locked — can't be opened from the outside without a key. But maybe I didn't mention the firewall between that stairwell and the rest of the building."

"So if they did get in that window, they'd be sealed off." It was actually a question but I tried to make it sound like fact.

"Right," replied Viejo.

"But what if they crawled around that little ledge and came in one of these rooms next to the fire escape?" asked Doc.

"Then we're screwed," said Viejo. "Once they get into any resident's room, they have access to that hallway and then to the rest of the building... except the elevator, which is down and open."

"I'll go see where they are," said Doc.

"No," I said, sounding more like a plea than an order.

"Why not?"

"We need to stay together." It sounded logical. "If we split our firepower between two floors, something might happen... and we wouldn't even know what."

"Well, we can't just sit here and wait for them to come trotting down the main staircase," he said, sounding more snarly than he'd likely intended.

"How about—" My phone vibrated loudly and all five of us jumped twelve feet, including Viejo in his wheelchair, Sylvie on her walker, and Tureen with her space-age hip. "Uh, hello?" I said.

"Ma'am, it's Captain Lionel. I was told you're expecting me. Didn't buzz the door 'cause I didn't want to scare anybody, but you need to let us in. We just saw somebody break a window on the east end of your second floor."

"Viejo!" I blurted out. He knew what to do. The rear door's lights turned green and we heard the rumble of boots and elbows and clanking weapons. "Everybody inside, Captain?" I yelled down the hall.

"Yeah, all eight inside. Secure that door."

Viejo was way ahead of him.

"What part of the facility are you in, ma'am?" asked Lionel, but I heard his voice in the hallway a half second before it was transmitted on my phone.

Stuffed the phone into the purse I was wearing like a sling and called out, "Around the corner. Don't shoot. Only friendlies here."

He still stopped at the edge of the control room door and jabbed his face quickly in and back out. "Clear!" he grunted and then stood in the doorway as his seven men fanned out in the lobby in front of us.

Doc told him we suspected one of the convicts was inside upstairs, but we hadn't had a chance to go look for him. The captain nodded, sending two of his men to check the upper floor.

"Most of the residents are in the cafeteria," I said, pointing to my left. "We have one staffer and a janitor with them. These three," I said, indicating Viejo, Tureen, and Sylvie, "are also residents..."

He motioned for two others of his team to check on the cafeteria folks. "Where's the hatch to the roof?"

Viejo pointed to the spot on the framed evacuation floor plan and the captain sent two other men up the inside stairs. His pistol still out, the captain squinted at Doc. "Who's the one with the trooper rig?"

I nearly lost it again. Every time I thought about Todd and Denny being gunned down, it hurt even worse. While I collected myself, Doc introduced himself and explained about my ill-fated security detail. Then he came over and hugged me.

"The feds will recover those bodies for you, ma'am," said Lionel. "That's one thing they're real good about." The captain was tall and broad, with skin nearly as dark as the black of his SWAT uniform.

"Are you here to reinforce or evacuate?" asked Doc, who'd heard most of my conversations with the governor.

"Once we got inside, I was supposed to assess the situation and report back to the governor directly." A diplomatic non-answer.

"Captain," I asked, "if you'd had no specific orders, what would you likely do here?"

"You have elderly residents here, some of whom can't easily be moved?" he asked.

I nodded.

"In the absence of orders, I'd be inclined to keep your position from being overrun."

"Did you bring any snipers?" asked Doc.

Lionel struggled to suppress a grin as he shrugged. "All my guys are snipers." But he went on to clarify they'd been ordered *not* to engage the primary group of convicts or endanger any hostages. That clicked with what the governor had emphasized to me. "Now, ma'am, what's the rest of your situation here?"

I did my best to explain... quickly.

Then Lionel darted over to the front windows, where the lieutenant had been observing and counting.

"Only four out front, all armed," said Lt. Staubach.

"We lost track of the other guy," I said, "unless he's upstairs with the one who made it up that tree."

Viejo nearly jumped out of his wheelchair. "Got him!" And he pointed excitedly at the monitor showing the east stairwell. "He must've come in through the second floor end window and realized he couldn't get inside, so he's down on first floor now."

After quickly signaling the lieutenant to keep monitoring the convicts out front, the captain hustled over to the console. "If he's in that stairwell, why doesn't he just waltz into the hallway?"

Viejo explained how those doors, when locked, only opened to exit but not to enter.

"Why didn't they just break a window on first floor?"

Another explanation, Viejo showing as much pride in the indestructibility of the first floor's windows and doors as if he'd designed them himself.

Lionel received a transmission on his collar mic, evidently from the pair he'd sent up to second floor. "Understood, Team One. Hold your position." Next he spoke into his collar piece and the two men from the cafeteria came trotting over. He briefed them quietly and they sped to the inside exit door of the east corridor. "Okay, what can this guy do inside that fire escape?"

"As I understand it," I replied, "he can only run up and down the stairs."

Viejo nodded. "No way to get inside the main facility, so the only other thing he can do is leave through that external door."

No longer hugging (though I keenly felt the absence of his strong arms), Doc and I intently watched the monitor showing the view from the emergency stairwell camera.

The captain's single sharp whistle got the lieutenant's attention and he evidently knew what his commander wanted. Staubach held up four fingers.

"Okay, four still out front and one trapped for the moment," repeated Lionel. "First priority is the single loose target and my guys have him pinned down upstairs. Second priority is the stairwell dude. Hang on." He confirmed something with the two on the roof. Then, evidently addressing the pairs on second and first floors, he transmitted orders through his collar piece. "Teams One and Two, engage. Affirmative. Engage."

CHAPTER 14

GUNFIRE UPSTAIRS, TWO single shots which sounded alike and one long burst from some weapon that sounded entirely different. On the monitor, we saw the stairwell convict react to those shots on the floor above, and he urgently headed for the outside door. Before he'd done more than touch the emergency exit release bar, the two downstairs SWAT guys zoomed into the stairwell, conked him, disarmed him, and dragged him, semiconscious, into the hallway.

"Secure that door," said the captain, pointing down the long corridor.

"Doesn't it automatically lock back?" asked Doc.

"Not if it's opened from the inside," answered Viejo. So he reset the switches — and both lights burned red again.

"Okay, two targets under control. Now let's see how much they know about what's going on in this burg." Lionel started to dash off, but heard something on his collar mic and turned around. "Is the elevator broken? My guys can't call it up."

"I'll turn it back on." Viejo punched a console button.

While Lionel was checking on his two operational teams and their captives, the lieutenant remained glued to the front windows and seemed to be communicating with some of the men — likely those on the roof who would also be focused to the south.

We five who had already been there re-gathered around the control room's console. "Wow," I said. "These SWAT guys are super efficient."

Seeing in real life what they'd likely only viewed on television, Tureen's and Sylvie's eyes were wide with wonder. Behaving as though they witnessed such operations every day, Viejo and Doc both smiled and nodded.

At the windows, Lt. Staubach spoke into his collar device and three seconds later the commander was by his side. Then Capt. Lionel hurried over to us.

Before he could say anything, I blurted out a question which had bugged me since they'd first arrived. "How come, with such a small squad, you guys have two officers?"

"Ma'am, we don't officially exist yet, which is to say, we're not declared operational until after some additional certifications, inspections, and reports. Besides, we're still a very small outfit. In a normal SWAT unit, the officers would be back at headquarters and there could be six or eight teams of six or eight guys. An experienced sergeant would be leading each team."

"Well, your team is quite efficient, considering it doesn't officially exist."

"Yes, ma'am," replied Lionel with a sweaty smile. "We're tight." Then he eyed the front windows and got us to refocus on the reason he'd trotted over. "When they heard gunfire in here, those four perps took cover behind the fountain. We're not positive, but they seemed to be waving at somebody else outside."

"There's a *seventh* convict dogging us?" I asked, groaning.

"Not necessarily," said the captain. "None of us spotted anybody else. Besides, maybe it wasn't actually a wave. Anyhow, when they didn't get any further signal from one of the two inside guys, one of those outside punks split off to head back south, presumably to communicate with other prisoners elsewhere."

"Not good," said Doc.

"What does that mean?" I asked.

Lionel eyed his watch and grimaced. "My lieutenant thinks Convict Four is going back for reinforcements."

"Oh, crap," I said.

Doc nodded solemnly. "Even though they certainly heard your gunfire, those thugs outside couldn't know that we have a SWAT team in here now. So they still think they're gonna waltz in, rob the place, and maybe play footsie with that young office-building girl."

The captain's expression first suggested he agreed, then his eyebrows arched. "What girl? The governor just said old folks, a few employees, and you, ma'am."

I explained how we'd spotted Britney and how we'd gotten her from there to here.

The elevator dinged and two SWAT guys dragged out the convict who'd been loose upstairs. He was alive and conscious, but had a leg wound and maybe an arm wound — difficult to tell with all the blood.

"Where's the nurse station?" asked one of the two escorts.

Viejo pointed almost directly overhead, basically the area they'd just departed.

"Bullets went clean through, no bones broken," reported the SWAT corporal. "We'll stop the bleeding and keep him from going into shock."

Doc grabbed the captain's sleeve. "It makes no sense for them to be hanging around Verdeville still, but…" Then he explained what we knew about the late Mrs. Pollard.

Lionel whistled. "That complicates things. Some convicts do obsess over the people who helped put them away."

"Any info about the breakout from the two convicts you captured?" I asked.

"Very little so far," replied the captain. "But we haven't had time to interrogate them properly. Neither knew anything was going to happen. They were just delighted to be free and were looking for a vehicle to steal, to get out of town with… so they say."

"They didn't get very far," said Doc. "Do you believe them?"

"Neither one seems bright enough to conceive of a complicated plot, but I'm guessing there was enough scuttlebutt that they had at least an inkling their transport would be detoured. As to why they've waited here with that payback character, I don't have a clue."

"Some convicts form close bonds inside," offered Viejo.

The captain eyed his watch again. "Look, ma'am, my orders are to get you and get out."

"I can't leave while these unprotected seniors are stuck in here," I replied. "Especially if there's a chance of more convicts heading this way."

Lionel frowned. "The governor isn't going to like that."

"I know, but it won't be a surprise. I've already told him two or three times."

"We've got to report in," he said tersely. "What do you expect me to tell him?"

"Tell him there are more convicts than we thought and they nearly have us surrounded." *A small fib.*

His eyes narrowed. "Won't make any difference. We have absolute, strict orders to get our team out before the federal response establishes its perimeter. This is their designated turf now."

Doc protested: "As long as you don't actually interfere with the feds, just being here shouldn't be a problem."

"Our status is still provisional," replied Lionel. "We haven't been certified by somebody in Washington who needs to put a few checkmarks on a computer screen. If the feds knew we were on-scene as a uniformed operational team even for a minute, they'd freak and the president would have the governor's balls for breakfast." He paused, looking a bit sheepish. "Pardon my language, ma'am."

"No problem. I've heard…"

My phone vibrated and everybody jumped except the captain. I'd never realized how loudly and harshly it buzzed on that setting. "Hello?" It was Gov. Ampersand, asking whether the team had arrived, the status of the convicts outside, et cetera. I answered completely and truthfully.

"Let me speak to the captain."

"Hold on, Governor." I covered the mouthpiece and soundlessly asked the captain, with my lips over-forming the words, "You want to talk?"

Lionel made a stretching motion with both hands, which I interpreted to mean *stall the governor*. So I did. And while I stalled, the captain and lieutenant huddled in front of the control room's open window and whispered. Lionel slapped his subordinate's shoulder and trotted upstairs, presumably toward the nurse station.

Then the lieutenant came over, accepted my proffered phone, and punched the speaker button. "Governor, this is Lieutenant Staubach." If he were in Hollywood, he would be typecast as a corn-fed all-American college football athlete. "The captain is interrogating our two prisoners in another area at the moment. Can I help you?"

"Yes, Lieutenant, the ETA for the federal response team is imminent. You know I risked my office putting you guys in there. Now grab Mrs. Temple — tie her up if you have to — and get out quick. That's an order."

"Yes, sir, I understand. We'll do everything we can to comply, but there are two complications."

The governor's brief silence sounded like steam was pouring from his ears. "What exact complications, Lieutenant?"

"First, one of the outside convicts deployed back to their primary zone and is expected to return with armed reinforcements. We don't yet know how many, but we anticipate being surrounded within minutes. Second, your lieutenant governor is a stubborn woman, and she's armed." He winked at me.

"Damn it, Lieutenant. You're trained to take out any uniformed enemy, plus terrorists... but you can't handle one stubborn female?"

"Sir, I have to go. More gunshots outside," he lied. Disconnecting the call, he handed back my phone. "That's the best I could do."

"Will there be trouble over this?"

He shrugged, evidently prepared to take the heat.

I didn't know how to respond, but remembered an unrelated question. "Did anyone ever say who that admiral is?"

Staubach's eyes widened. "I thought they'd already told you."

I shook my head slowly as Doc edged closer.

"She's a big muckety-muck in Homeland Security. These convicts found a bargaining chip that gives them plenty of leverage."

"Could they have known she was in that annex building this afternoon?" I asked.

Doc chimed in. "Like I told you, no general or admiral goes anywhere without a dozen people being notified."

But the lieutenant governor can travel to Verdeville and nobody knows but me. "But how would the bad guys find out? I mean, whoever planned this prison bus breakout."

"That's above my pay grade, ma'am," said the lieutenant, "but every bureaucracy has a few loose bolts and there are lots of criminals or enemies out there listening for the rattle."

"So re-routing the prison buses and letting out all those convicts was not the goal of this operation," said Doc with as much authority as if he were conducting the briefing.

Capt. Lionel, having just returned to the control room, responded. "It's still likely at least a small handful of particular prisoners were important to the planners of this op. And when they discovered the admiral was here, just off their bus route, they realized the conditions were perfect. About four dozen convicts scattered all over downtown Verdeville as decoys and the bad guys and their few ex-prisoner cronies in the catbird seat with the admiral and some guards." He tugged at his belt and the heavy Kevlar vest, redistributing some weight. "Our wounded prisoners say this small group's leader — Mister Payback — is named Largo. It would surely help if we knew who organized that larger picnic with the hostages."

"I don't know his name," said Doc, "but my money's on that guy in the play performance room."

"Who?" asked Lionel.

"Sat right by the door in a bad suit, and looked like he didn't want to be there," I added.

"Yeah," said Doc. "He got up to leave right before you did."

"Where did he go?" asked the captain.

"No telling," answered Doc, "but it was hardly a minute later that the fireworks broke out."

"Did it appear he was in communication with anyone?" asked Lionel, gesturing to his collar mic.

Doc smacked his own forehead. "I knew there was something else! Yeah, he was messing with his cuff and kept moving his hand to his ear, like he was rubbing an itch on his face."

"Must be their inside man," said the captain. "Ma'am, did you observe anything else about him?"

I hadn't even noticed those hand movements, but that might have been because my eyes were more on the man in the Ike jacket, Doc Holliday. I just shook my head.

The captain grabbed Doc's shoulder and told him to give his best description of that suspect to the lieutenant to call in so it could be relayed from the governor's office to the feds.

"Won't they wonder how the governor found out?" Doc asked. "I mean, supposedly the feds don't know she's here... right?"

"Right," said Lionel, nodding. "Good point. We'll have to manufacture an anonymous citizen who saw that suspect on his way up to the annex performance room."

All this cloak-and-dagger business about not stepping on federal toes was absurd, but I decided to pick my battles. And right now that main conflict was with the remaining convicts just outside Elderwood... plus whoever was likely joining them from the larger group.

"So any news or guesses about their demands?" asked Doc.

"We'll probably learn more about all that from CNN than we will from the federal team," said Capt. Lionel. "But right now we've got a bigger problem. We're ordered out of this facility before the feds set their perimeter. And that's in how many minutes?" he asked Staubach.

"Uh, the governor said imminent, whatever that means," the lieutenant replied.

He checked his watch. "So let's be out of here in twelve or thirteen minutes, tops... and we still have to hump it back to our vehicles."

I'd already told everybody I would not abandon these seniors, so I didn't bother to repeat it. *But perhaps the SWAT guys had come prepared for an evacuation.* "What did you bring?"

"Two Humvees — reinforced outside and modified inside."

Not enough space for everybody.

"Where'd you leave them?" asked Doc.

"A few blocks north, on the southwest corner of that big park," answered Lionel. "Didn't want anybody to see them — convicts or federal officers."

"Are you taking those two prisoners with you?"

"I'll double check with my superior," replied the captain, "but I'm already certain we can't. If we show up in Nashville with orange jumpsuits from Verdeville, the feds will definitely know we were here."

"So what do you plan to do with them?"

He held up a gloved finger. "Stand by." Then he pulled aside the lieutenant and they conferred privately.

While the two SWAT officers were debating, Doc moved close to me and whispered, "They've got no choice. We'll hold the prisoners."

"We have to keep them restrained and confined." I turned to Viejo. "Does Elderwood have any small, secure spaces we can lock up tight?"

"We have a room I call the brig," he said, smiling at me. Then he faced Tureen and Sylvie. "Remember old man Canker?"

"He passed, bless his heart," said Tureen.

Sylvie nodded and grinned, showing partly loose dentures. "Oh, I understand." And she explained to us. "Mr. Canker wouldn't stay in his bed at night, so they finally had to strap him in."

"Which room?" asked Doc as he motioned wildly to get the officers' attention.

"The brig is Room 1-10," Viejo replied, pointing slightly to his right. "They had to move Canker where the night clerk would spot him if he got out. But he was so sneaky, they later added the restraints."

While Doc filled in the lieutenant on our new cell for the two re-captured convicts, I pulled Lionel aside. "Captain, how much trouble…"

More gunfire outside! Convict Largo had shifted to high gear.

CHAPTER 15

AT THOSE SHOTS, which sounded like a mix of rapid semi-auto bangs and several bursts from an automatic, everybody ducked. The two officers raced to the front windows as they chattered on their collar mics. Doc followed.

Evidently leaving one SWAT member guarding the two prisoners, the other three from the capture teams zoomed into the main waiting room and crouched behind their officers. Presumably the other two good guys remained where they'd been this whole time, on the roof.

Lionel urgently whispered something to Doc, who hurried back over and crouched down by Viejo's wheelchair. "Looks like things are about to heat up, and the captain wants you and the two ladies to help calm things down in the cafeteria."

Tureen and Sylvie were already in the hall, but Viejo had started shaking his gray head before Doc even finished. "Sorry, no can do."

More shots from out front and Doc took off again. I placed a hand on the old man's sturdy shoulder. "It'll be a lot safer, Viejo."

"I've fought enemies a lot stronger and smarter than this pack of escaped thugs," said Viejo as he stroked the sleeve of the borrowed Ike jacket resting over his shoulder. "I was on the front lines in Italy — Messina, Salerno, and Anzio. It was a Nazi shrapnel fragment from an 88-millimeter blast that slowly ground a divot in my spine over the next fifty years. I'm not going to transfer to rear echelon now." Then, apparently sensing that his tone had sounded too sharp, he added softly, "Besides, when I do reach my earthly end, I'd much rather go out fighting."

My throat swelled up and my eyes grew moist. If we'd had time, I would have hugged the stubborn old fool. But Viejo just wheeled his chair back toward the console, pulled a snubby revolver out of his lap pack, and laid it on the counter near the keyboard.

When he saw my eyes widen, he put a finger to his lips. "Shhh! I don't think anybody knows I smuggled it in here."

"Well, they're bound to notice if you start shooting."

Viejo paused to calculate. "If any of those thugs actually make it through this SWAT team and you two with weapons," he pointed first to me and then to Doc, standing not far away, "then everybody will be glad I bent a stupid rule."

"Them getting in depends partly on how determined they are," I suggested.

"No," said Viejo, "it's mostly a matter of whether these SWAT guys have rigid rules of engagement."

I'm sure I looked puzzled.

"Sometimes law enforcement is hobbled by bureaucrats who shoot off emails by the minute but who never fired a weapon in their lives," he said. "Sometimes an officer has to take direct fire before he can legally un-holster his own weapon."

I positioned my hands like I was holding one of the SWAT weapons — a real assault rifle, not a civilian AR-15.

"Yeah, I know, they're armed to the teeth, but I'll bet there's somebody at headquarters counting their cartridges when they get back."

The SWAT guys were intently watching the building's front — not much else they could do through bulletproof glass.

Several times Doc had scurried over near the front windows, but was repeatedly waved back by Capt. Lionel. Finally he gave up and settled in next to me. He saw Viejo's revolver immediately and pointed. "What's that?"

"If anybody else asks, it's a cigarette lighter," he replied, grinning. "But to you, it's a Chief's Special. Smith and Wesson."

"Five-shot .38 special?" asked Doc.

Viejo nodded proudly. "Bought it new in the fifties. It's one of the first commercial series."

"Sweet," said Doc, looking as though he'd start drooling.

More shots from out front. Largo had to keep his small, loyal cluster busy. From our side, only watching and waiting.

Doc and I rushed over to see what was happening, but we stayed well back behind all the black uniforms. As best I could determine, all of the original four convicts were at the fountain, but had been joined by at least three others that I could see. Several had obviously stolen civilian clothes. "They still don't know we have reinforcements, do they?"

"Probably not," replied Doc. "They'd be crazy to take on this team."

Using his collar mic, the captain checked with his roof men and repeated to us — and the other SWAT men around him — what he'd been told. "There's a blind spot near the rear exit area..."

"Presumably that's clear," I said, "according to the console camera."

Lionel continued, "...one convict at each side door, and another somewhere in the rear."

"So they really do have us surrounded," I muttered.

Doc hugged me tightly and whispered something consoling. Didn't catch the exact words because I was too startled by his embrace. And even in the stress of our situation, I found myself wishing I could be in a more comfortable position so I could more fully appreciate his physical gesture. I hadn't had this much contact with a man since Arnold had stormed out in his patented narcissistic huff thirty months ago.

More gunfire and then a pause. Finally a loud voice — obviously Largo's — called out, "We don't want no trouble, man. I just have a little payback errand to take care of. So unlock these doors and let us in. It's gittin' a little chill out here an' we don't have no jackets." Largo punched the guys next to him as though they all shared a hysterical joke. "Just let us in and give us a sandwich, man."

A few more shots at the front doors and windows, though none broke through the strong materials used in the first floor's over-built construction.

When the firing ceased, Capt. Lionel received another update from the roof men and relayed it to us. "During that last burst, two more cons from out front went to the sides. Not sure exactly where, but my men are redeploying to the other corners to see if they can spot them."

It seemed to me Lionel should deploy a few more men up to the roof, but I kept my own counsel. I scurried back to Viejo at the console. "Have the exit door cameras picked up anything unusual?"

"Not yet, señora. I don't think anybody's gotten close enough to the doorways yet."

More gunfire from out front, but the bursts seemed lazy, almost like the men firing were already bored with their endeavor. *A diversion obvious even to me.*

The captain replied to a question from a roof colleague. "No, do not take them out. Repeat, do not engage." Then to us he said, "We want to see what Largo has in mind. My snipers could put them down, but then we'd have dead bodies to explain. Let's wait another—"

Boom! An explosion from the back door stunned everyone, and several of us staggered.

"Back door breached!" yelled Viejo. "Panel light green."

"What do you see?" shouted Lionel as he motioned two of his men to head that direction.

"Smoke," replied the old man, pointing to his console screen. "Only smoke. But I heard it with my own eyes."

"That was more than a concussion grenade," observed Doc, his eyes wide and alert.

"Most likely some C-4," suggested Lt. Staubach.

"Go," said Lionel to Staubach, who jumped from his crouch and raced toward the rear entrance.

Lionel was already receiving information on his collar piece. "Repeat," he commanded, and paused.

"What's going on?" I asked.

The captain held up a forefinger and spoke additional orders into his collar mic.

Doc seemed to know what was happening, but before I could ask either of them whether any convicts had entered our facility, my phone vibrated and I jumped again. Yanked it from my heavy shoulder purse and recognized the number — Governor Ampersand.

CHAPTER 16

"Yes, sir, what news?" I asked the governor, trying to sound like I wasn't about to scream.

"One extraneous tidbit about that admiral. Supposedly one of her nieces is in the play. The admiral was in a big Nashville meeting when she was asked to attend."

"Guess that explains why she was in full uniform," I added, feeling way too jittery for a chatty conversation. "Doc said admirals don't usually travel alone."

"Apparently she was," said Ampersand, "unless you spotted somebody with her."

I didn't remember anyone... certainly nobody in uniform. *Right now, I just want off the phone so I can find out what's going on in the back.* "Maybe they were waiting outside at her staff car."

"Julia, is that gunfire I hear?"

Good ears... it wasn't on speaker. "It's been sporadic for these past couple of minutes. And just before you called, there was an explosion at the back door."

"Explosion?"

"Yes. I've heard two possibilities," I explained. "Maybe concussion grenade or possibly C-4."

"Plastic explosive," he said with a heavy groan, as though he'd been inside the blast zone himself. "Where's the SWAT team leader? I've been trying to reach him."

"Right here, Governor, rushing back and forth. But he's pretty busy at the moment."

"I need to speak with Captain Lionel immediately. And when I do, you're going with them A-SAP. No excuses and no delays. I can't allow my lieutenant governor to get blown up or shot down in Verdeville." He seemed to think of me more as a breakable office possession than his state leadership teammate.

I couldn't think of anything to say that wouldn't blow back in my face.

No convicts appeared from the blasted rear door and no additional firing came from out front. Perhaps the south-side thugs were waiting to see if their own guys would open the front doors and wave them in.

"Julia, I know the captain isn't more than a few feet away from you," said Ampersand brusquely. "Give him your phone. Now. That's an order."

In truth, Lionel was about seven feet away, one eye on the front windows and the other watching for someone to return from the rear exit. Crouching over, I scooted to the captain and handed him my phone. "It's for you. The governor."

"Lionel here," he said, and remained silent and stony-faced as the governor chewed him out. "Sorry, sir. Yes, I understood your previous instructions. No, I'm not being... No, sir. I understand. Yes, sir. Will do. Yes. Yes, sir. Immediately. I understand." I'd never seen a face as dark as his turn suddenly pale, but the captain was definitely shaken as he ended the call and handed back my phone.

"Feds are coming right away and you've been ordered out?" I guessed.

He nodded, checking his watch.

"And the governor insists you bring me with you?"

"Yeah," replied Lionel. "Cuffed and stuffed, if necessary... says your boss."

"Don't even think..."

"Relax, ma'am. I'm not going to force your evac."

"What will happen to—?"

He interrupted. "But I do have to pull the team." He swallowed hard. "That's not negotiable. If I don't, all these guys will be out of a job. If we're caught violating our pre-operational status, our unit might very well be suspended before we're formally activated."

"I understand, Captain." Doc having just returned from checking on the back door breach, I sensed him beside me again. Even his proximity was a comfort. "The governor called." I told Doc everything.

He also understood, and looked like he wished he were leaving, too. "We caught a punk climbing through the busted door," said Doc, motioning over his shoulder with a thumb. "Well, they did... the lieutenant."

As if he'd been cued, Staubach appeared from the hallway to the rear exit. "Captain, one got away. Door was blown off the hinges... they knew what they were doing." Right behind the lieutenant was a SWAT corporal clutching a limp convict. "This one had an AK-47," he said, holding it up like a trophy. "I left Sergeant Tuck guarding the open doorway, and here's our newest prisoner." The thug looked dazed and terrified. Wrists cuffed in back, black tape across his mouth.

"Secure him with the other two," said Lionel to the corporal. "When you come back, bring all three of their firearms and we'll stow them safely in this office." When they'd departed, Lionel continued with the lieutenant. "See if he knows how many reinforcements they got and whether they expect any more." Then he clutched Staubach's sleeve. "And find out where they got that C-4."

Staubach whooshed away like a ghost on steroids.

On his collar mic, the captain spoke to his sergeant, guarding the demolished rear door. Of course, I couldn't hear Tuck's replies, but from what Lionel was saying, they were discussing how to barricade the door and whether to make it temporary or permanent.

I was actually up to speed on this part. If they blocked it up really well, they wouldn't be able to leave through our currently most advantageous exit — namely to the north, out of view of the convicts in front. But if they only blocked it slightly, then the bad guys could easily swarm in after the SWAT team left. It was the only time since his arrival that I'd seen Lionel hesitate.

It was time for an executive decision. "Block it with enough cover for your guard, Captain, but the barricade needs to be light enough for us to get out quickly. That could be our only exit if things get rough out front."

"Yes, ma'am," he said, smiling. "That's the right call."

Outside, Largo resumed shouting. "We don't plan to be here when those black choppers show up, man. So you've only got a few minutes to make up your minds before we bust in and shoot everybody. Besides, we got us a bazooka thing on the way and that'll loosen up this front door."

"I wonder if they actually have a LAW," whispered Doc.

Even I knew that was a light anti-tank weapon... but only because of movies I'd seen. I turned to Viejo. "Besides the janitor, is anybody here healthy enough to help with the barricade?"

"Glover can't talk worth a hoot and he looks like a scarecrow," answered the old man. "But he's as strong as a state fair bull."

I'd already forgotten about Glover. "Okay, have Heather send them up here and the captain will tell them what he needs."

He made the call over the public address. Then to Lionel, Viejo said, "We've got more of those tables we used on the cafeteria windows. They'd cover the whole width of that doorway... and almost the complete height."

"Pretty sturdy?" he asked.

"Won't stop rifle bullets," replied Viejo, shaking his head.

"How about three stacked together?" The captain held up that many fingers.

Viejo grinned. "It'd surely slow them down."

Lionel spoke into his collar mic — presumably to Sgt. Tuck at the exit. "Sturdy and secure, but we need to be able to quickly move it from our side."

Right away, the janitor appeared with an apprehensive Glover, and the captain directed them down the corridor toward his sergeant. Doc followed along behind.

No point in further worry about the door barricade, but there were other pressing matters. I knew the SWAT guys had already been on-site considerably longer than they'd anticipated. It had been assigned as a quick in-and-out grab, with a hurried departure. "Captain," I said, tapping his elbow, "how long before your team absolutely has to withdraw?"

He checked his watch and exhaled heavily. "Absolute max of fifteen, ma'am, but we really ought to be moving fast in under ten. Which means I need to break off and brief the men A-SAP." Speaking into his collar mic, Lionel stepped off to the side, where he could keep an eye on the front windows.

It was only a matter of moments before the lieutenant and three others reappeared, presumably leaving one man on the roof, one guarding the prisoners, and Tuck at the rear exit. They formed a tight cluster around their captain.

I couldn't hear any of his initial, extremely brief announcement, but I knew he was explaining the governor's withdrawal orders. All protested, and Lionel silenced them sternly. "The order is *stand down*. If this unit has a future, we've got to follow legal orders."

The lieutenant evidently raised the issue of morality, but Lionel quashed his objection. He repeated his order and the huddle dispersed suddenly, each man on his collar mic — presumably to the other three team members.

Capt. Lionel returned to the control room window and leaned against the wall where he could monitor the front windows. "They weren't too happy."

"So I could see," I replied. "But I believe I understand the governor's decision, in light of the federal task force heading this way." Well, I didn't understand it, as much as I recalled seeing Hollywood renditions of it — the feds always totally ran their own show, without local assistance, which they considered interference.

Slowly his team assembled. Snipers from the roof, guards from the prisoners' holding cell — six in all, surrounding the captain. Only Sgt. Tuck remained at his post at the rear door. After Lionel whispered a few last-minute instructions, his team headed down the hallway toward the exit, then began running double-time as soon as they'd cleared the breeched doorway. I watched on the rear monitor.

When Lionel stepped into the control room and exhaled noisily, I extended my hand. "Thank you for coming, Captain. Tell the governor it was my fault."

His dark-gloved hand held mine, but he didn't squeeze. "You can tell him, ma'am. I'm staying."

CHAPTER 17

I SPUTTERED MY surprise, but so much relief was mixed in that my eyes leaked. "What do you mean, you're staying? The governor ordered you out."

"He ordered the *team* to stand down," he replied as he watched the windows. "And they've withdrawn. I've sent them home."

"But what about you?"

He shrugged as his fingers stroked the shoulder stock of his modified M-16. "I'm on vacation. I've just relayed my leave request with Lieutenant Staubach."

I jumped to him in a clumsy embrace, mostly blocked by all his equipment, firearms, and Kevlar. "Will you lose your job over this?"

"I'm entitled to vacation days," he replied as calmly as a man could with a female lieutenant governor hanging onto him. "Sometimes the paperwork takes a few hours to catch up."

When he cleared his throat, I realized I had to release him.

At that moment Doc reappeared around the corner and stared suspiciously.

Is that jealousy in his eyes?

"Uh, Captain," said Doc, "your team is gone and we've replaced the tables. Who do you want guarding the door?"

I stepped in. "We need Viejo here on the console. Heather and Britney are helping the cafeteria group. The only other able-bodied people are the janitor and Glover." I didn't mention Tureen and Sylvie, who'd been helping but in non-combat ways.

"Okay, use Glover and the janitor," said Lionel. "We've collected a few bad-guy guns. Can either of them handle a firearm?"

"Not Glover," replied Viejo, "but Wally served in Vietnam. He can shoot."

Lionel fingered the pistol in his holster — looked like a Glock — and replied, "For the time being, let's consider them lookouts only. Unarmed." He motioned toward the office corner, where the confiscated weapons had been stowed. "Let's consider those as emergency, last resort. We sure don't need any gun accidents by civilians. If those rear guards see anybody coming, the janitor races up the hall and tells us here." Then he pointed.

Doc sprinted toward the cafeteria to brief them on their way to the rear exit.

The captain eased up to the front windows, spoke softly with Sylvie, who had resumed her position off to one side and was still stoically leaning on her walker. *She must have difficulty getting up and down, or surely she'd prefer to sit.* He positioned Tureen, however, in a chair at the juncture of the main hallway with the rear exit hallway. From there, she could see both the east and west inside doors, the barricade, us in the control room, and would know if anybody poked their heads out of the cafeteria.

Doc was back within seconds and joined me and Viejo in the control room. When the captain re-entered, I took a deep breath. "Okay, it's basically up to the four of us to keep this facility secure and protect these folks."

From out front, revenge-minded Largo resumed loud invective to get our attention, then shouted, "I've got some personal business with one of the old biddies in there, man, but I've promised my good friends here that we can also have a quick party before we head out. We already spotted one girl and we figure there's also a nurse or something inside. Won't be long before a rocket takes out that door. But you still got a few seconds to cooperate."

"It sounds like the bad guys are getting impatient," observed Doc. "Did your men get anything out of the prisoners?"

"Doesn't really help our immediate situation here," replied Lionel, "but that last guy said most of the prisoners had drifted south, some to Highway 70 and some toward the interstate. They'll stick out, of course, but presumably they figure to hijack some vehicles and get as far away as they can."

Doc looked in a southerly direction but couldn't see much besides the bank of reinforced windows. "Any idea how many are doing that?"

"That guy would only be guessing, but I'd estimate not more than a third. I figure another third will dissolve into the residential neighborhoods or hit the woods. There's a lot of forest land around this little town."

"Did he know anything about the planners of this breakout?" I asked.

"The small number of inside guys — evidently the ones intended to be released — are very rough customers. None of our prisoners claim to recognize any of the outside people who'd apparently organized it."

"Anything about the hostages?"

"The admiral and some of the guards are still alive. No word on their condition. The prisoners have no idea why they'd want a naval officer... unless it's for her, um, uses as a woman."

I shuddered. "Lieutenant Staubach told us she was connected with Homeland Security."

Lionel nodded. "That was in our briefing, but not much more."

"Still no contact from the hostage holders?" I asked. "No demands?" I realized it was rhetorical, because none of our party could possibly know.

"This could be one of those cases," replied Lionel, shaking his head, "where you have to watch the TV news later to figure out what happened and why."

"Okay, okay." I held my hands out flat. "Nothing *we* can do for them anyhow. And they're obviously the main focus of the federal task force, which should be here within about..." I raised my eyebrow at the captain.

"Let's just say soon."

"All right. So what's our plan, here, until the feds seal up everything at the annex?"

Doc responded first. "I don't think we can count on a speedy resolution to whatever those criminals dreamed up. Since they nabbed an influential admiral, I'm betting they want some TV coverage at the least. No telling what their agenda is, but it could last for hours."

The captain had been nodding. "Right. You can expect the negotiators to spend time assessing the principals, trying to defuse the situation, and bargaining for release of the hostages. That eats up a lot of time... might run through afternoon and night."

"So what do we do here?"

No immediate reply, as each of us briefly retreated to our own thoughts.

From out front, more loud cursing from convict Largo. "We ain't gonna be extra nice once we finally git inside, man." More invective. "Since you missed your chance to give us a good welcome. You're runnin' outta time."

The vengeful bad guy's threats worried me, but I had to focus on our defense. "Ideas?"

Then Viejo spoke up. "I'm guessing the majority will want to treat this like a siege and protect the fortress." He squirmed in his wheelchair. "But I've got an idea we ought to go on offense. In a military engagement, we'd send out a patrol and nab another prisoner."

The captain was shaking his head. "Too risky. Only three of us are armed and mobile. We'd have to send at least two. Who would stay? And what happens to the rest of you if our patrol is ambushed?"

"Good points," I said to Lionel as I patted Viejo's shoulder. "But I like the idea of *doing* something. Not just waiting for either an enemy assault or a federal rescue."

"To me," said Doc, "the main issue has always been to get out of the area that's been overrun."

A familiar refrain, and I wondered if Doc had finally decided to turn tail.

But he continued, "As long as Largo and his gaggle are outside wanting in, these folks are in jeopardy."

"And even if there weren't any bad guys trying to get in," added Lionel, "once the federal team gets its perimeter established, there won't be any civilian movement in or out."

Viejo grumbled, "I still say nab a prisoner. Lure them away from the group one at a time and jump them."

"Hey, that gives me an idea," I said as I tried to suppress a nervous giggle. "Luring them is the key."

Three sets of eyes focused on me intently.

"Yeah. That guy Largo is out there counting down the seconds. When he gets to zero, let's open the front doors."

CHAPTER 18

―⚜―

"OPEN THE DOOR?" said Doc, eyes wide as saucers. "Julia, are you nuts?"

"*Invite* them inside?" asked the captain, shaking his head.

Viejo grinned. "Ambush."

"Right," I said. "They've been yelling for us to let them in, but they probably didn't really expect it. So we just open the door and see how many we can nab."

The captain was immediately up to speed. "It'll be tricky because we can't fire any shots. That would warn the others away."

"Oh, okay," said Doc. "You mean we hide behind the door and clobber them."

"Well, it needs to be more artful than that," I said. "We need to lure the rats in far enough that the others can't see or hear what happens to them."

"For a good rat trap," said Viejo, "you need bait."

"Didn't Largo mention food earlier?" I asked.

Everybody nodded.

"Okay, we'll set up some food on a table and invite them inside."

"You think they'll fall for that?" asked Doc.

Lionel motioned his dark chin toward the front. "They don't look particularly bright to me."

"Let's do it," I said. "Viejo, get Heather up here. Doc, rustle up a table. Captain, you work out the logistics of where to place the table and where you and Doc need to be to conk them. I'll brief Tureen and Sylvie and we'll pull them back to the cafeteria out of harm's way. Viejo, you brief Glover and the janitor... uh, Wally."

Viejo issued the buffet preparation instructions on the P.A. system and wheeled out of the control room toward the rear exit.

It shouldn't take long on the food because the residents had been snacking almost since we'd arrived at Elderwood.

From outside, Largo began with his customary curses then again announced their imminent attack on the front door.

"Captain, stall him," I said. "Tell him the old lady is dead but we're about to provide some refreshments before they get on their way out of town."

He rolled his eyes. "What was her name?"

"Mrs. Pollard."

Lionel did as I asked, and it bought us a bit more time.

Our plan was solid. And things came together so quickly, I was honestly surprised. In any meetings at the state capitol, we'd have spent hours arguing and jockeying for position, looking for favorable angles and calling in markers. But this — the Elderwood campaign — was a prime example of cooperation during a stressful crisis, and it was glorious to experience.

Within moments, the table was arranged where it would be in sight of the front porch once the doors were opened. Doc was stationed at one side of the front double doors with his pistol and a small sign he'd hastily drawn. I hadn't even had a chance to read it. Viejo, in his wheelchair, was safely behind the control room's counter. The captain stood in front of a utility closet off the side, barely in the east hallway.

Our bold plan was simple. But would it work?

Largo, the convict leader, had just announced his revised time warning when I pushed the door open just a crack and called out, "Don't shoot. I'm opening the door. I have an announcement."

"Sounds like a woman!" shouted one convict.

"Shut up," said Boss Largo. "Hold your fire, man. Let's see what this witch has to say."

"Okay, I'm opening the door slowly and I need your attention." I waited a second to steel my nerves. Pushing one of the double doors about halfway open, I held it as still as I could with my trembling hand and yelled, "You said you're hungry. We have refreshments available on this table. Like my coworker just told you, the lady you wanted passed away a couple of months ago. Our other residents are old and feeble and have nothing of value. Come inside and have a quick snack... then you can move on before the federal negotiators seal off this whole area."

"Hey," yelled a convict, "she's no witch. She's a looker."

"Who *are* you, lady?" asked Largo. "And what are you doin' with these old folks?"

"Just visiting my sick aunt," I lied. "Nobody here wants any trouble, Largo. We've put the food on a table in this front room. Just come in and eat... then move along."

"How do you know my name?"

"We, uh, bumped into one of your buddies after he knocked on the rear door."

He comprehended and flashed a partially toothless grin. "Why shouldn't we stay a while?" he asked. "You know, get comfortable and relax, man. Maybe get to know you a bit."

"Plus that other girl who went in the side door," added one of his buddies, poking with his elbow.

"Shut up!" barked Largo.

"Everyone here is secured in our safe room, so we won't be available to entertain," I said boldly. "But you're welcome to these refreshments. We just ask that you not linger because our residents have nap schedules."

"So where's that fancy safe room, lady?" asked Largo.

"You don't need to know, but it's in the basement," I lied again. I seriously doubted we could actually lure anyone that far from the main entrance, but it would be a great ambush spot, so it was worth a shot.

"I'll send in a buddy to check out this food table," announced the leader, "but if there's any funny business, man, he'll shoot you full of holes."

"None of us will be here." My third lie in the past few seconds. "I'm leaving right now for the safe room. Bye." And I let the weight of the door pull it back 'til it was propped open only by the width of the *Reader's Digest* issue Lionel had just then handed me before he waved me back into the east hallway.

On my way, I signaled Viejo to duck down even farther in his chair and roll out of sight.

Doc was poised just inside the door with his borrowed pistol in one hand and the homemade sign in his other. I couldn't make out the hurriedly scrawled wording.

Lionel positioned himself in the doorway to the windowless utility room, and kept motioning me to sidle farther down that hallway.

The seconds ticked by.

Doc's eyes suddenly got really big. He dropped the sign to the floor behind him and raised that hand with two fingers extended.

"Two enemy approaching," said Lionel with a hiss. "Change in plans. Stay here, ma'am." And he hustled to the other side of the door. Doc could surely have handled one, but not both.

My belly iced over again. I retrieved my own borrowed pistol from the purse which had rubbed an irritated rash along the path of its strap — on one shoulder or the other all this time since we'd left the annex. Would've been a great day to wear slacks with pockets that held a wallet. Would've been a terrific day for flats instead of heels. And a fantastic day to stay the heck out of Verdeville.

When Doc took a deep breath, I knew the two convicts were close. Lionel held up his hand — a clear signal to wait for his command. The door pulled open slowly. I had to take a breath, but only a shallow one. The door opened a bit farther and a convict stuck his head inside. Lionel and Doc both flattened silently to the wall beside the double doors. When the first convict spotted the food table and lunged on inside, his companion followed with no hesitation. The door slammed behind them, and Doc whacked the one nearest him with the barrel of his pistol.

The captain took the other in a choke hold so fast that the man never made a sound. His eyes bulged and his face turned bright red as Lionel disarmed him and whispered something urgently. Clutching at the captain's strong arm against his throat, the thug managed to provide a satisfactory response.

When Lionel released his grip slightly, Doc held up his sign for the thug to read, then pushed open the door slightly with one foot. Next, the captain shoved the convict's face into the opening. "Tell him," hissed Lionel.

"Food... looks... good," he read weakly from the sign.

From my vantage point in the hallway, I could not see through the window blinds, but it sounded like the other four bad guys had jumped up and were ready to scurry inside. But Boss Largo halted them. "Hold on. Something's fishy." Then he called out, "Hey, Homme, where's DeAndre?"

No reply from the man in our doorway because Lionel yanked him back, conked his head, and let him fall to the floor like a sack of stale horse feed. Then he kicked away the magazine issue, pulled the door to, and signaled Viejo to re-lock it from the console.

Doc dragged his inert convict to the utility room, where Lionel met him with the one he had by the scruff of his orange jumpsuit's neck. Both were zip-tied, wrists and ankles, and their mouths taped. Lionel took their weapons to the office where the others were stowed.

I finally took a breath. "Why'd you lock the door again? There's still at least four more goons out there."

"The jig's up. Largo knows his guys were ambushed."

Doc nodded. "Looks like we're back to siege and fortress."

"Maybe not," called out Viejo, as Largo and his diminishing gang resumed firing at our bulletproof front windows.

"Maybe not what?" I asked as I hurried — nearly doubled over — to the control room.

He pointed to one of the console's screens. "Take a look."

Just then Wally the janitor appeared at the large office opening and announced breathlessly, "They're back!"

I grabbed his shoulder. "Who?"

"The SWAT guys!" he said, before hurrying back to the exit to help tongue-tied Glover pull away the barricade.

"Hang on," said Viejo as his thick finger jabbed at the monitor. "They're still armed to the teeth, but now they're wearing *civvies*."

CHAPTER 19

SWAT GUYS RETURNED? *If only true!* I couldn't see enough on the monitor, so I hurried down that short hallway and helped Glover and Wally wrestle the last of the three tables from the door.

Lionel and Doc were still at the front looking out, and instinctively ducking back with every new *pow* of semi-auto rifle fire against the shatter-proof windows.

The final table down, Lt. Staubach burst through the doorway like a fullback breaking through an unmotivated scrimmage team. "Everybody still okay, ma'am?"

"Safe and sound. Two new prisoners since you left. Welcome back, Lieutenant." My impulse was to grab him in a bear hug, but I restrained myself. "You were ordered out." And only a few minutes ago. *I could never change clothes that fast.* "What happened?"

"We couldn't leave all these old folks here. Sergeant Tuck commandeered a nearby school bus and I've routed an EMT van for the people in motorized chairs."

They had done more in a few moments than some state employees accomplished in a month. "You mean we're switching to evac after all?"

"Yes, ma'am, if y'all hurry. Those feds are heading downtown right now. We should be hearing the choppers pretty durn quick."

"How can I help?"

"Get on the P.A. and have everybody who can move on their own file down this hall and we'll escort them to the bus. I'll get with the captain about the ones we'll need to carry."

"What about the bad guys out front?"

"The captain's call."

So we had only a handful of minutes to evacuate a stranded office worker, some Elderwood employees, and 27 seniors — including a bed patient, an assortment on scooters, motorized chairs, and regular wheelchairs, plus several others using walkers or tripod canes. *Wonderful.* The evacuation suddenly seemed more complex than clearing the beaches at Dunkirk.

Doc appeared behind me with a sweaty, strong arm around my shoulder. "Don't worry, Julia. You've got this."

I had no time to waste on being emotional, but my eyes were filled with tears as I gave the instructions to Viejo, then raced to the cafeteria to be sure everybody was moving. They were — with surprising efficiency and almost no complaints.

More gunshots to the front of the building. I crouched over and scurried to Lionel and his lieutenant, discussing strategy to one side. "What's the plan, gentlemen?"

The captain slapped Staubach's shoulder and sent him racing toward the bus, EMT truck, and two Humvees, all parked close behind the facility. "Basically we need one sniper to pin down those guys out front and buy enough time for everybody else to concentrate on the loading."

"Let me guess," I said. "You're the sniper."

He nodded. "I'll be on the roof. When you load the final resident, somebody will alert me and I'll climb down the outside ladder to that little shelter over the rear door. I can jump to a Humvee from there, if they've parked it close enough." He checked his watch again. "We don't have much time 'til we hear rotors, and not much more while they're setting up, to be completely gone. Can you handle everything down here?"

"Yeah," I said, lying to both of us. "Got it covered." Actually I'd been running on adrenalin for the past hour plus. The only time I'd been off my feet was while I was kneeling on the rough pavement outside... and later while Doc cleaned and bandaged my skinned knees. The heavy shoulder bag was becoming my worst enemy, and my toes were screaming from the too-elegant-for-commando-work heels.

Lionel sprinted toward the inside stairs and within seconds I heard rifle shots from the roof. Peeking out the notch in the front window blinds, I could see it was only suppressing fire. He was aiming into the fountain in front of them... splashing them with cold water, but making no attempt to injure any.

For my money, he could've shot them dead — one and all — but I understood the SWAT team's footprint had to be minimal.

Viejo was still in the control room, frowning while monitoring the console screens as I approached. "What's wrong now?"

"Maybe nothing," he replied, "but I was trying to keep a head count as they loaded."

"And?"

"Thought for a second there was an extra head…"

"Everybody's moving so fast," I suggested, "maybe you counted somebody twice."

"Probably so."

"You'd better get rolling while there's still room in one of those vehicles," I said.

"Not worried, señora. I'll go out when you do."

I could hear occasional single shots from the roof, but no return fire from the four convicts out front. Lionel's suppression was working.

I hadn't had a chance to check on the loading of residents, so I inquired.

"I couldn't see all that much with the range of our rear entrance camera," said Viejo, pointing to a monitor. "But except for the EMT guys handling those few residents with no mobility at all, it was a bit like two strong men loading hay bales."

"Meaning?"

"Fast and efficient and not an extra second for chatter."

Wished I could've seen that. "But still gentle, I hope?" Yeah, it came out like a question.

"Let me put it this way, señora," he said, lacing his fingers loosely, "They had only a few minutes to save about thirty people from getting shot or killed. You might find a bruise or two tomorrow."

Small price. "Have you seen Doc?"

"Everybody under age sixty has been loading the residents and the captured weapons." Viejo pointed with his thumb toward the rear exit and parking space.

"Any thoughts about what to do with our five prisoners?" I asked.

"Well, let's see. There's two in the utility room with zip ties on their hands and feet. In the brig, one is zip-tied and two are basically harnessed to beds. All five are gagged."

Yeah, that wide black tape came in handy. "So how do we get *them* out?"

He looked shocked. "We don't. Those last two probably won't even regain consciousness 'til supper time." He pointed to a paper tablet. "I'm leaving a note taped to the control room window which gives the two room numbers and the number of convicts in each."

"For the feds to find?"

Viejo nodded.

"How will they know to look for escapees in Elderwood?"

"The last thing I do before you and I vamoose is call the biggest TV station in Nashville. I give them an anonymous hot tip about five orange suits seen entering the retirement home but never coming back out."

It finally dawned on me that Viejo had two distinct voices: one like the actor Ricardo Montalban with more than enough cultured accent to sound smoothly sophisticated, and another like typical banditos in Hollywood movies. This conversation, like most, had been in his first voice. "You think they'll follow up?"

"Of course they will. It's probably the only inside information they'll get during this whole standoff. The feds will have everything else clamped down tight."

I had the heavy feeling I was overlooking something. Looked around the control room. Patted the pistol in my shoulder bag and eyed the revolver in Viejo's lap. "You'd better put away that gun or you'll be tossed out of Elderwood for policy violations."

Just then Doc burst in, grabbed me in another sweaty embrace, and said, "Let's go, Julia. Everybody else is loaded up."

Viejo made his call to the TV station. No wasted words.

My brain screamed with the stress. "You sure the cafeteria is clear?"

"Just came from there," replied Doc.

"What about the girl from the office?"

"Britney's on the bus. Everybody's accounted for. Let's go."

"Viejo, is there a speaker on the roof for this P.A. system?"

He nodded slowly. "One in the central stairwell. If that door is open, which it should be, maybe he can hear it."

"Okay, tell Captain Lionel we're the final three and we're heading out now."

As Viejo made that announcement on the public address, we heard two more spaced shots from the roof. No way to know if the captain had heard us.

"Where is he shooting from?" I asked.

"He's on the front edge," replied Doc, "firing south into the fountain."

"He won't hear us calling from the parking area in back," I said. "We need some way to signal him. Ideas?" Nobody would believe this unless they've been in the middle of a convict crisis with live fire heading their way, but I'd totally forgotten I even owned a cell phone. Apparently the others had, too. I took a breath and spotted the wall clock. "Hurry."

"Roman candle," said Viejo suddenly.

"What?" Doc and I asked nearly simultaneously.

"Leftover from Cinco de Mayo. I kind of borrowed it from the box."

"Where is it now?" I asked, as I wondered what had happened to the firecrackers I'd never used.

"Top of my closet," he replied. "Actually too high for me to reach."

"I'll go," said Doc. "What room?"

"Room 1-13," he said, "east corridor, second to last one on the left."

"You two get going and I'm right behind you," shouted Doc as he raced down the hall.

With Viejo's strong arms propelling his wheels, he didn't need me pushing from behind, so I was basically hanging on for dear life. Sgt. Tuck and a corporal lifted Viejo from his chair and carried him into a Humvee backed near the rain cover for the rear door. The bus, EMT van, and other Humvee were already lined up along Hickory Street behind Elderwood. *Everybody clear.*

I grabbed Doc's Ike jacket from the wheelchair. As I was about to climb in the Humvee, Doc emerged from the back door, tossed the Roman candle up to Staubach — standing on the vehicle's roof — and said, breathlessly, "Fire that off to let the captain know we're ready."

The lieutenant tossed it back down to Doc — and with sweaty face and plenty of teeth, he smiled.

CHAPTER 20

Smiling? The lieutenant was smiling? There could be no smiling during an evacuation of seniors when your captain's on the roof shooting at armed bad guys. I was stunned.

"What's going on?" asked Doc.

Staubach pointed to his collar mic, clipped to his civilian shirt. "Dude, we're in constant contact. The captain knows more about what's happening down here than you guys do."

Lionel appeared at the roof's edge, made a hand signal, and received one back from the lieutenant. Then he slung his M-16 over one shoulder and positioned himself at the ladder's top as Staubach and Sgt. Tuck aimed their weapons at either end of the long facility.

No convicts appeared around the corners, so they'd apparently been sufficiently cowed at the fountain.

"Well, tell the captain that I'm firing south, over the building," said Doc as he pulled from his shirt pocket the butane lighter I'd returned.

"What's that for, Doc?" I asked.

"Just a bit of extra distraction for the bad guys... to give Lionel safer egress," he replied.

More like Doc saving face.

He wedged the end into a divot and leaned it against an edging stone for the proper angle. Before the Roman candle was halfway through its cycle, Lionel had scampered down. The captain and Staubach jumped into the Humvee with Doc, Viejo, me, and our driver, Cpl. Billup. Normal Humvees are four-seaters, but this one had a double jump seat rigged to the rear cargo area. It wasn't roomy for two full-sized men, but it would do for Doc and me. Lionel joined Viejo on the middle seat and Staubach rode shotgun.

Sgt. Tuck ran toward the Humvee out front. Everybody situated, our corporal sped off and joined the other vehicles. After the panic and adrenaline of the afternoon, I felt almost giddy, and the Roman candle's red and blue explosion over Largo's fountain was icing on the cake.

We could just hear the rotors of multiple helicopters, doubtless the federal task force, to our distant west, en route to Verdeville. "Choppers pretty much on time," said Staubach.

"Actually, a couple of minutes early," replied the captain, "unless they plan to circle the target area for a bit."

I didn't care what they did... other than hopefully rescuing the surviving hostages and retrieving the bodies of those brave law enforcement officers who had done their duty and paid the ultimate price. We joined our ad hoc convoy — Humvee One in front with five SWAT guys, EMT vehicle next with four non-ambulatory residents, school bus with all the other residents and the Elderwood staff, and our loaded Humvee bringing up the rear. While we were briefly lined up, Sgt. Tuck finally reached the Humvee at the head of the column and became the sixth occupant when he jumped in the middle seat area. From what I could see, he didn't even appear to be winded.

"Where's the office girl?" I asked as our convoy began moving together, heading west along Hickory Street, which somewhat separated the old north residential area from the newer subdivisions farther north.

"She's on the bus," said Staubach, "helping with the old folks."

Viejo had been counting on his fingers. "I've lost track, but I think I've counted forty-one heads."

That sounded about right to me. "How many should we have?"

The old man shrugged. "I thought it was forty."

"Better one extra than one short," I concluded.

"We got everybody loaded," added Doc. "And plenty fast, too."

As I handed Doc his jacket, Viejo's eyes followed it reverently.

Doc noticed. "It's my grandfather's," he said. "Otherwise, I'd let you have it."

"No, no, señor," he said. "Even then, I couldn't accept it." He swallowed hard. "But it's been an honor to hold one again for these few minutes."

Don't know why I had a lump in my throat.

His own eyes cloudy, the captain punched Staubach's shoulder lightly. "When did you guys cook up this bus scheme?"

"While we were changing into our civvies in the Humvees at the staging area," answered the lieutenant. "Tuck called a friend who drives a high school bus in this burg. Turns out he lives on the far side of this park... so he wasn't more than six blocks away."

"You were supposed to report back to headquarters," said Lionel, trying to scowl.

"Right you are, Captain," replied Staubach, "but we all decided to join you on vacation."

Lionel removed his glove and extended his hand. "There could be some trouble..."

"We've been through worse," said Staubach. "But we're a team."

The driver, Cpl. Billup, added, "Besides, sir, as you keep telling us, officially we don't even exist yet."

I was greatly relieved to be unharmed and to have seen these deserving seniors safely evacuated. I knew the federal task force would handle everything else, including — hopefully — the safe rescue of any hostages and a dragnet to recapture all the escapees. Yet still I wondered what the criminal planners had hoped to gain from all this.

Cpl. Billup had been listening to a Nashville radio station and turned it up so we could hear an update about the conflagration in Verdeville. Their newsflash quoted unnamed sources from the governor's office, saying the entire escape had been engineered by a South American drug cartel who wanted one of their North American distributors out of prison. That report, cautioned the announcer, had not yet been officially corroborated. Then the announcer cited a TV station bulletin that some convicts had somehow trapped themselves in a downtown retirement complex. The residents of that facility were believed to have fled.

If I'd started laughing, I would've cried. And in fact, I did a bit of both.

Doc pulled me close and wrapped a muscular arm around my back. His fingers tightly gripped my arm like he didn't plan to let go.

He was a sweaty mess, but I didn't have the heart to mention it. And somehow it didn't seem to matter. "Sorry you stayed, Doc?"

He thought a moment. "No, just ashamed I acted so skittish at first. Guess my focus was too narrow."

Except for the driver's, all other eyes were monitoring us, though they pretended to be admiring the scenery zooming past our Humvee windows. I snuggled into Doc's embrace and closed my eyes for the second time that afternoon. "We came out okay."

"Better than okay."

I wasn't sure what he meant, but didn't know how to frame the question. My silence was his prompt.

"Because I finally got to meet you again," explained Doc.

Looking down at my skinned and bandaged knees, I tried to smooth out some of the uncountable wrinkles in my way-too-tight-for-skirmishes skirt. "You didn't exactly catch me at my best."

"Actually, I believe I did."

I'd never been good at responding to compliments and wasn't even sure how he meant it, but couldn't force myself to inquire. So I jumped to a different rail. "This long-ago meeting you keep talking about. Did it really happen? Or is this just some really bizarre pick-up line?"

"It happened. End of May... I was still a junior." Then he mentioned the year.

"Oh, yeah. I'd just graduated. That was my first summer as Dad's intern."

He nodded. "You already had an early tan." He motioned toward my legs — presently quite a bit paler than they were fourteen years before.

As I pondered where our conversation might be heading, I also realized I had no idea where our convoy was traveling. But I knew we'd be safe, so I decided to leave that in Capt. Lionel's capable hands. "Wish I could remember your particular class."

"Nothing especially notable about us," Doc replied. "Which is one reason I was so impressed that you took the time to explain your father's absence, convey his apologies to us — and make it sound sincere — and then even discuss the bill he'd been called back to Washington to vote on."

The end of that May had been my second week on the job. And it was possibly the first time, of many others over those four summers, that I'd had to stand in Dad's stead. As I recalled now, I must have gone on instinct. But if it stood out to a teenaged Doc Holliday, I couldn't minimize it fourteen years later. "Well, that trip to the capitol is an important part of high school civics."

The four eavesdroppers evidently found humor in my attempts to sound detached, and Staubach couldn't restrain his grin.

Seemingly able to ignore the other individuals riding with us in such close quarters, Doc continued his reverie. "During your briefing, you were standing right next to me... so close that I could've touched you if I'd dared reach out." His hand now made that movement.

I grabbed his hand and held it gently — not actually as restraint, but more like I needed to inject some reality into his adolescent flashback. Then, still trying to sound stern, I said, "The capitol police would've been on you like fleas on a dog. You can't grope a senator's daughter."

"Maybe not, but I sure wanted to touch you."

When my face heated, Viejo struggled not to laugh and I shot him a caustic squint. "Well, Doc, it sounds to me like hardly more than physical attraction for the first city girl you saw outside of Verdeville." I'd intended it to sound lighthearted but then worried it might have come out harsher.

"No, not all physical," replied Doc cautiously. "Though it certainly included how pretty you were. Uh, are." After adding the gentlemanly amendment, he cleared his throat.

"Seriously, I'm honored that my presence in Senator Temple's office, um, helped make your visit memorable, but I still don't understand why it's stuck in your mind all these years." I wasn't fishing for compliments; I was really confused.

"It's not like an obsession," he explained. "In fact, after you went off to college and I later saw in the paper that you'd gotten married, I basically forgot about you."

Somehow that hurt my feelings, albeit retroactively. At times like that, you wish for a quiet spot with low light... and not being crowded into a rumbling Humvee with four other nosy people.

We finally broke through the residential area well west of downtown, turned south on Highway 231, and headed for the interstate.

"But when I saw you today at the annex, it took me right back to that year." Doc shifted in his seat and hugged me even tighter. Evidently the crowding spectators didn't bother him at all. "You were so mature, so grown-up, so responsible..."

Hadn't felt that way — not back then and not much even since.

"...and most of the girls I knew were giggly goof-offs, selling fries and burgers."

That tall teenaged boy from Verdeville had fallen in love with me!

"And earlier today, seeing you in that audience and knowing you're divorced now, I had a crazy thought maybe we could — somehow — pick back up where we left off."

But there was nothing to pick back up. I hadn't even known a teenaged Doc Holliday was in that office! *And fourteen years later, how do I handle this man's vulnerable heart?* Plus, why did it have to be in front of an eavesdropping crowd while hurtling down the highway? Didn't know what to do or say, so I did what nearly every politician does — I turned the awkward moment into a question. "Where did you figure it would go at that point, Doc? I mean, assuming we lived through this experience... which we have."

He shrugged. "Not sure. Maybe dinner?"

"Aw, go ahead and kiss her," said Capt. Lionel, nudging Doc's leg in a brotherly way. "Nobody's watching." He lied, of course. Even driver Billup was monitoring us in his rear view mirror.

Before Doc could do anything besides look sheepish, a phone rang and all six of us jumped through the reinforced Humvee roof.

CHAPTER 21

NOT MY PHONE, however. It was Capt. Lionel's. After he answered, he put it on speaker and we all heard the governor's voice. With no exchange of pleasantries, Ampersand demanded a status report.

The captain explained we were safely away and told him about our five prisoners left behind. "The federal choppers just passed over our heads a few minutes ago."

"What's all this crap about my whole dang SWAT team taking a sudden vacation?" demanded the governor.

"Just taking advantage of the nice weather, sir," replied Lionel, "before it turns too cold."

"Listen, Captain, I know full well you and your men deliberately disobeyed my orders."

Lionel started to protest, but the governor halted him. "And I'll let it slide this once since there are supposedly no dead bodies to explain and, as far as I know, the feds didn't spot any of you." Ampersand paused to gasp more hot air. "But what kind of footprint did you leave? Nothing can be traced to the SWAT team we don't have."

"Some duct tape, a few zip ties," said Lionel. "Oh, and if anybody checks, they might find a couple dozen shell casings on the roof. But we recovered the ones from inside."

The governor had noticeably cooled down in seconds — the art of a flexible politician. "Maybe we'll get lucky and it'll rain or snow before anybody finds them."

"Yes, sir. We're counting on luck."

There was a short silence, which I interpreted as Ampersand wishing he had more to complain about. "Now let me talk to the lieutenant governor."

The captain handed me the phone. I accepted reluctantly because I really didn't feel like being chewed out. "Hello?"

"You got out in one piece, Julia?"

"Yes, sir. It took longer than we'd intended, but all the residents have been safely evacuated."

"Good. When you count their family members, that's worth at least two hundred votes next election." Ampersand sounded more cynical than he'd likely intended.

"Thanks for sending your SWAT guys, Governor. Without them, we'd still be under fire and trapped."

"Yeah, well..." He stammered at my compliment because we both knew he'd ordered the team to stand down.

"Governor, we heard a radio report just now that a major drug cartel set up this whole thing just to spring somebody from prison."

"It will be hours before we know anything official," he replied.

My blood was running high. "Governor, is that report true?"

Ampersand replied with such diplomatic side-stepping that my only certainty was that he'd denied nothing.

Rolled my eyes. "Can they trade hostages for a convicted drug distributor?"

"Julia, that's out of my hands. Decisions like those go all the way up to the attorney general and likely the White House. Maybe the Pentagon, since there's an admiral involved. Suffice it to say the negotiators will do everything they can to defuse this without collateral damage... and in the meantime, the feds have their own commando teams who will be figuring the angles for a resolution that's, um, un-negotiated."

I gulped.

Then his voice mellowed slightly. "Have you still got me on speaker?"

"Yes, sir."

"Well, this part's for your ears only, Julia."

"Okay," I said, punching that button, "speaker's off."

"Julia, you disobeyed my repeated direct orders. But you made a brave on-the-ground decision and by all accounts behaved courageously. Who knows what would've happened to those retirement home resident voters." He cleared his throat in that soft politician fashion. "Your father would've been proud of you, Julia."

Tears rolled down my cheeks and I couldn't swallow the lump to reply. Doc hugged me tighter.

"But this is important. We can't let people get the idea our state leadership travels unprotected and nearly gets caught in hostage traps."

"Todd and Denny were on duty with me, but they were overwhelmed by numerical force and superior weapons. Ambushed and killed." And remembering their bloody bodies made me shudder.

"Yes, I know... and that's a separate matter. We'll get their remains back to their families, with full honors." He paused again and shifted gears. "For your part, we've got to spin a totally different story to the media and the task force."

"Lie to federal investigators?" When my body stiffened, Doc released his embrace and gave me some space in the crowded Humvee.

"No," said Ampersand, "if they ask direct and specific questions, we certainly have to tell the truth. The trick, Julia, is to steer them away from those questions."

"Governor, that's ridiculous. People have seen me! At the annex, in the nursing home, and possibly some of the Verdeville citizens peering out their windows from behind locked doors. I can't pretend I wasn't even there."

"Julia..." Ampersand was using the voice he probably saved for his grandkids and other minors.

I took a few deep breaths. This was not the time or place for my shouting match with the boss, and when we did have that conversation I didn't want any witnesses. The governor obviously had a motive for scrubbing me from this Verdeville mess, and I was betting it had to do with continuing to keep me out of the public eye. After all, he'd been violently against the constitutional adjustment which resulted in my being elected. For the time being, I'd ignore the *why* and just go with the flow — his flow. "How do you expect me to fake not being there?"

"You never reached Verdeville today. You'd intended to go, but something came up. Maybe Aunt Tilly got sick. You work out the details."

I mulled over his lame and idiotic fib. "That's your lie for the media?"

"Right. Once the media starts reporting something, usually the feds accept it as fact. So it mainly has to sound convincing to the reporters and producers. Who do you know at the Nashville affiliates?"

"Nobody, really. Just a few faces I saw on the campaign trail."

He seemed shocked. "You don't have any regular contact with TV reporters?"

"Sir, I'm practically invisible in the capitol. I'm excluded from almost all the important meetings and the only assignments I get are garden teas and flower shows. I don't think I've seen a TV camera since the election." I decided not to soft-pedal my doldrums.

"Okay, I understand. And you're right." He took it well. "I haven't been exactly open-armed since you came on board. Fact is, I didn't know what to do with you."

Painfully obvious. "I'm part of your state leadership team, Governor. Let me be your partner."

Another slight pause as though he were visually checking someone's expression in his office — or down in the basement crisis control center, wherever he was at that point. "Okay, I will, Julia. We can fix this. But right now the important thing is to erase you from this Verdeville mess. You weren't ever there."

"That'll be tough to sell to the residents and staff. Not to mention the office girl we rescued." I tried to remember anyone else during that trying time. "I understand your position, Governor, and I won't be out on the streets tooting my horn about how I spent this afternoon. But I'm not going to lie about it either."

Since that word always made him cringe, I was sure he was doing so now. "What about newspapers? Any editors or reporters who will listen to you?"

"Well, I know some people who trusted and respected my father. Maybe they'll give me a chance."

"Get to them. Tell them version B of this afternoon and see if it'll stick."

"Can't do it, Governor. The best I can do is tell them — off the record — that I was in the annex when it was attacked and we took refuge in the Elderwood. And I'll ask them to keep it off the record because it likely affects my, uh, future security arrangements." *And probably my future career.*

He paused long enough to play it through his head twice. "My way is simpler and easier to manage."

"But it's based on a lie and I know those will always come back to bite me."

Silence.

"Governor?" I thought he'd hung up on me.

"I'm here." He sighed heavily. "Okay, we'll play it your way. Meet with at least one newspaper and one TV station — both at the same time, so you have a witness — and tell them what you just said. But get them to look you in the eye and swear it's off the record."

"I can request it, but can't compel them. If they determine the public has a need to know the truth, I'm sure they'll spill it."

Ampersand ignored me; perhaps he had external influence he could exert. "And set up that meeting for this afternoon, before the six o'clock news."

"I'll do my best."

"Okay, Julia. That should be plenty. I guess I underestimated you after all. You've got a lot more of your old man in you than I would have imagined, considering the packaging is so different."

He'd buried a vague compliment in there, but somehow it felt more like a leer. I shook it off. "I think we both need and want a better working relationship, Governor, and I pledge to do my part as best I can recognize it."

"All right, Julia." He made no reciprocal pledges. "Now get that meeting set up, pronto. Bye."

CHAPTER 22

———✥———

As I disconnected the governor's call and handed back Capt. Lionel's phone, Doc leaned over and whispered, "Everything okay, Julia?"

I sighed heavily and laid the side of my head against his firm chest. "I guess so. It's not like I was going to campaign on my participation in that valiant stand against armed convicts—"

"Though you certainly could," interjected Doc, with a wink at Viejo.

"But I wouldn't," I continued. "And now my very presence in Verdeville is being politically erased."

"I only heard your end, but it was easy enough to guess what he was saying. The governor's finally realizing you're a lot more of a leader than he gave you credit for... and he sees you possess more courage and honor than he does." Doc's hand brushed some of the errant hair from my face. "And he might even view you as potential competition."

I shook my head at the competition part. "For years, people have been telling me I have no executive potential, and when I finally show some spark, the governor hurries to blow it out."

"Don't let him hold you down," replied Doc. "I'll bet Ampersand wishes he'd been the one here evacuating those old-timers... complete with TV cameras running. I think he's jealous about what you did to save those folks."

"What *we* did. You, Viejo, these guys in black Kevlar. Heck, even Heather and the janitor. Everybody pitched in." And all gallantly remained silent as I spoke.

Then Doc added, "Don't forget Tureen and Sylvie... plus that strong guy."

"Glover," I stated.

"Right," said Doc. "And even the guy in the windbreaker who helped load some of the less-ambulatory folks onto the bus."

I hadn't noticed that individual. *No matter.* "Exactly. The whole miracle of this afternoon was that several unlikely individuals came together as a smooth-working team and we all got out safely. I believe that deserves some recognition... and our citizens need more feel-good moments like this."

"Yeah, especially with the bad news at the annex building... starting with those bus guards and your troopers, and ending with the people watching that little performance upstairs."

I quietly wondered how that full Broadway-bound production could move past this, but perhaps it would generate even larger audiences once word got out that some half-dozen of their principals had been murdered — not to mention the playwright and director.

Another phone rang, making everyone jump again. This time it was mine — and I couldn't even remember when I'd switched my phone back from vibrate. It was intern Kayla from the governor's office.

She apologized for bothering me and explained her errand would normally be handled by Charise, her boss, or by Helen, my own secretary, but...

"It's okay, Kayla." I interrupted. "What's the message?"

"A reporter just called, hounding me for info on your whereabouts. He got wind of a rumor that you were stuck in some office building during this fracas in Verdeville."

"Which reporter and which paper?"

She provided both names.

"What did you tell him?"

"Nothing, Mizz Temple," replied Kayla. "The governor was up here earlier and said you never even reached Verdeville. What's going on?"

"It's complicated, but I'll have to explain later. I can't discuss it with the reporter yet, either. Right now I need you to set up a meeting at his editor's office for, um, four-thirty, and get at least one TV reporter there, too."

"Which one?"

"Doesn't really matter, but find a woman if you can. That gives us some balance."

"Everybody's running around covering that hostage situation in Verdeville," said Kayla. "What if they, um, balk at breaking off to meet with you?"

I had to think fast. "Tell them something vague but make it sound important." Suddenly my high school debate training kicked in. "It's an insider announcement from the governor's office. Exclusive to them, if they show up for it."

"Okay..." Kayla sounded like she was about to jump out of her skin. "I'm all alone up here. I sure wish Charise or Helen were handling all this. And I wish you hadn't gone to Verdeville, which you supposedly didn't get to, but reporters want to know why you're there."

"I know," I said, trying to sound calming. "It'll work out. Just set up the meeting and I'll explain things to them. And when I get to work tomorrow, you and I will have a chat. I know this is your first office crisis, Kayla, but you're doing just fine. All right?"

By the time we ended the call, Kayla sounded moderately settled. Still confused, of course. But that would be true for many people in middle Tennessee... with active shooters just east of Nashville, presumably dozens of dead bodies, hostages still in danger, criminal organizers with unspecified demands, dozens of convicts likely still at large, and a federal task force setting up its perimeter and negotiators. Yes, it would take time to rescue people, settle things, sift through the facts, bury the dead... and heal.

Doc watched me as I got all pensive. When I looked up, he smiled softly and hugged me again.

Having cleared the west end of Verdeville, going south on Highway 231, we'd just entered a westbound ramp onto I-40 when our convoy picked up a state trooper escort. "Captain, did your team coordinate this?"

"Yes, ma'am. Call it a combination of protocol and courtesy. They'll stay with our convoy 'til the evacuees reach the processing center."

"Uh, do you have a way of patching me through to them?"

Lionel signaled the driver, who handed over a mic, which the captain used to reach his own dispatcher. Within seconds, I was in contact with the head of Tennessee Highway Patrol District Three. It was a conversation I'd never wanted to have and hoped never to repeat, but I squeezed out the words necessary to inform him that Todd and Denny had fallen in the line of duty. When he asked for details, I had to give the mic to Doc. No way I could even list those bullet wounds.

After Doc signed off, he returned the mic to Lionel, who also conferred briefly with the district chief, likely about the convoy escort. After watching me silently for a moment, Doc asked, "How're you doing, Julia?"

"I'm tired." I dabbed my eyes. Suddenly the jostling of the Humvee and the silence of five people crammed about me seemed too awkward. So I patted my tummy. "And hungry, too."

"You think we could stop somewhere?" Doc asked Lionel.

The captain scowled. "We just reached the interstate a couple of miles ago. Unless it's a long run — which this isn't — it's much better to keep rolling 'til they reach the safe house." *Obviously the as-yet-unnamed processing center.*

"Captain, we've been breaking rules all afternoon long," I said. "Everybody's safe now. Can't we fudge on this *no stop* rule?"

"You're the second-highest ranking person in state government, señora," said Viejo. "Why don't you just order an override?"

It had never — not once — occurred to me that my tentatively-held elected position actually conferred any true authority. "I can't do that." If a male executive demanded something, it would be viewed as *decisive*, but a female's request could be seen as *bitchy*.

"Why not?" pressed Viejo.

"It's too... too... um, bossy."

Doc smiled but said nothing.

"However," I continued, "I could indicate an executive preference... and hope the people around me would not require an order to implement it."

After an exaggerated shrug, Lionel got on his collar mic and the Humvee leading our convoy — along with the trooper in his squad car — pulled off at the next exit. "We can't let any seniors off the bus or out of the EMT van until we reach our assigned destination, but the rest of us can dash in and bring out a selection of beverages and snacks."

It was hardly a moment later when the convoy stopped... but kept all engines running. "Ten minute breather and all the seniors stay put unless it's a restroom emergency," announced Lionel. He sent Staubach to notify the EMT van staff and to personally brief the passengers on the bus. Then Lionel, using his collar mic, told Sgt. Tuck in the front Humvee to further explain the delay to the state trooper in front of him.

Without me asking, Doc jumped out and hurried toward the convenience market to get me some refreshment.

The captain caught me watching Doc as he trotted away. "You two are good together, ma'am."

"Us?" My face warmed. "Oh, we aren't together."

Viejo smiled as he looked away, pretending to be watching the traffic zoom past on the nearby exit ramp.

Lionel frowned with confusion. "Oh, I thought you two are a couple."

"No, I'm recently divorced." Actually it had been about thirty months ago, after I'd thrown my hat in the ring for office, but before I'd reverted to my maiden name and then filed for office. "Doc and I only just met today... at the annex."

"Oh, okay." Still confused. "Well, none of my business anyway. I just thought..."

Then I remembered. "Well, now that you mention it, Doc says we actually met before. I guess you heard most of that. But we were practically kids; it meant nothing. It was more like sitting in your car at a traffic light and a guy pulls up in a truck. Yeah, you're four feet apart, but you didn't actually engage. I recall the situation he mentioned, but not the high school boy that later became Doc Holliday."

"No doubt it would've been more memorable for him," interjected Viejo, who'd given up pretending not to listen.

"Doc Holliday is a cool name," said Cpl. Billup. "Is he named after a gunfighter?"

"Don't know." I shook my head. "I've already asked, but he just said he'd explain later."

"He told me," said Viejo, and we all looked at him. "Doc got his nickname because he used to mimic that cartoon bunny."

I laughed. More than the explanation warranted, but likely because it broke the unrelenting stress. "Glad they didn't call him Bugs."

"So what's his real name?" asked Lionel.

Again I shook my head. "No idea. With everything going on, we never had time for proper introductions."

Lionel grinned from ear to ear. "Looked to me like y'all had been thoroughly introduced." Then his fingers made a motion evidently intended to convey our hugging.

To deflect attention from my new blush, I shifted gears. "By the way, where *are* we taking everybody?"

"The normal procedure would be to use one of the local churches or schools that participate in the FEMA network," replied the captain. "They used to be considered civil defense shelters."

"Good idea." I smiled. "I'd been thinking of a motel… and I wondered whose credit card we'd use."

Lionel looked puzzled and then grinned. "Yeah. At a motel they'd have access to a pool."

But he was right and we both knew it. The assigned shelter would have cots, blankets, food, and medicines… and hopefully, for these seniors, a nurse. Probably some temporary wheelchairs, too. Plus telephones for them to notify their kin. The SWAT dispatcher had likely made the arrangements and I was betting they'd selected somewhere in east Nashville.

Two large silver utility wagons zoomed past us and headed north on the narrow county road. *Don't often see twins driving bumper to bumper.* Plus they looked brand new. When I checked my watch, I realized I had way less than two hours to clean up and get over to the newspaper office. "So you're not too upset about us stopping here for a bit?"

"A few minutes won't make or break our schedule." Then he jumped out of our Humvee to personally monitor the five-vehicle convoy while it was stationary.

Capt. Lionel was a model of efficient leadership: decisiveness, action, courage, plus keeping his team members fully informed and involved. In his position, he was presumably able to use all his skill-sets; people respected and followed him because he inspired confidence. That was the kind of leader I wanted to be… that was the type of position I thought I had run for, the first time our new constitution allowed the office to be elected directly. Sure, I was youngish, relatively inexperienced, and underqualified, but I was eager to learn and willing to work. And the people did elect me! Gov. Ampersand, however, had decided it was easier to keep me boxed up in the capitol or on a short leash to garden parties rather than assign me actual responsibilities and let me learn. *Set me loose.*

After today, would anything be different?

CHAPTER 23

G<small>LANCING TOWARD THE</small> drab convenience market and wondering how long it would take Doc to return with my snack, I finally pulled off my heels — first time since late breakfast that I'd been able to wiggle my toes.

With Doc and the two SWAT officers gone, the Humvee held just me and Viejo... and our nosy but silent Cpl. Billup in the driver's seat. I moved from the back to the middle, next to Viejo.

Without the wheelchair, Viejo's arms and shoulders looked slightly lost. Not the most appropriate image, but it seemed one of his own components was missing. With his customized chair, he'd had a degree of mobility and independence not too much less than a person with functioning legs — except when facing stairs. But without his chair, perched as he was on the high Humvee seat, Viejo looked like a dependent old man. And until he was reunited with a wheelchair, he'd have to be carried from point to point. For a proud former warrior, that could be extremely difficult to deal with.

"Who's that?" asked Viejo, pointing.

I focused on the middle-aged man in a tan windbreaker, ambling toward our vehicle, and noted an odd smile on his face. "Don't know. Isn't he one of the Elderwood folks?"

Viejo's head moved to the left but before he could shift it back to the right, he stopped. "Not one of ours. But I spotted him earlier. He helped with loading people."

"Might be one of the SWAT guys." Without their gear and uniforms, they looked like regular people. "Corporal?"

"Yes, ma'am," Billup replied, turning toward me.

Tan-jacket guy was nearly at the Humvee window, so I whispered. "Is he one of your—"

Whack! The guy conked Cpl. Billup with something heavy and I lurched back, nearly knocking Viejo off his perch.

"Definitely not SWAT," said Viejo under his breath.

The limp corporal seemed unconscious but still alive as the intruder shoved him to the passenger side, swooped into the driver's seat, and faced us in the back. "Keep quiet," he said, waggling a pistol in our faces, "and maybe nobody gets hurt."

"This is nuts," I said. "There's a whole squad of SWAT men ready to stomp you into the ground. What are you doing?"

Viejo clutched my wrist, indicating I should be quiet.

"Shut up," demanded Tan Jacket. Then he wove his way over Billup's tangled legs and reached us in the middle seat. "Git up front... quick." He jabbed my shoulder. "You're driving."

"What?"

"Up front. Now. Quick, before they see anything."

When I reached for my purse, Tan Jacket made another menacing move with his pistol. "Now."

"I need my shoes."

"Now, lady. Or I shoot one of your pals here." He first eyed Billup in front and then Viejo, next to me. "This one's already a cripple, so maybe I should just put him out of his misery."

No response from Viejo except a cold stare he'd probably mastered during the slogging and bitter campaign in Italy.

"Okay, okay." I struggled past the intruder and plopped into the large driver's seat. I wasn't tiny, but the corporal was over six feet tall, so he'd had the seat way back.

Tan Jacket braced himself against the Humvee frame but didn't sit down. "Take off, lady. Now!"

"I can't even reach these pedals."

He poked the gun barrel into the right side of my neck. "Stretch. Let's go."

"Better do it, señora," added Viejo.

The engine had never been turned off, so I grabbed the stick, though I could scarcely reach the accelerator and brake with the tips of my bare toes.

"You're gonna wish you were driving, mister," I said. "I've only seen these in the movies." We lurched and the six-plus liter V-8 engine would've died if there had been a clutch. But this featured a three-speed automatic transmission and the only way to kill it would be to run out of gas.

"Get us out of here. Now." Another punctuation with the pistol barrel.

It was my first time driving a nearly three-ton vehicle that was seven feet wide — it felt like a small tank. As I pulled out of the convoy line, several faces turned our direction, including both SWAT officers, plus Sgt. Tuck and Doc — just then exiting the convenience store. "Look, mister. This is stupid. They all know we're leaving."

"Doesn't matter. Hurry up."

Nothing I'd done had stalled us very much. "Hurry up where?"

"Straight ahead. Get going."

"What's all this about?" I asked. "Who are you?"

"He's with them, señora," said Viejo, nodding in the direction of downtown Verdeville.

I knew exactly who he meant, but I thought we might gain something by compelling Tan Jacket to explain. "Them who?"

"You know who," replied Tan Jacket. "I sat outside your back door forever waiting on this gaggle to come out. Largo knew you'd make a run for it... which is why he told me to stick with you."

"Largo's involved in this?" I thought we'd left him hunkered down behind the Elderwood fountain.

"Different Largo," he said, and suddenly clammed up.

Hard to believe that prison held more than one Largo. "How many are there?"

"Never mind," replied Tan Jacket. "Somebody's waiting for us... and he really wants to meet you."

That sent a chill up my spine. "That's ridiculous. Nobody even knows I'm here."

"The boss does. Now shut up and drive."

Through my rear view mirrors, though not adjusted for my height or position in the seat, I could see Doc and the SWAT leaders conferring urgently. We'd only been gone a few seconds but I figured in a Western movie, Doc would've already jumped on the nearest horse and lit out after us. But this was neither a movie nor a Western. So they were evidently strategizing and probably consulting the Tennessee Highway Patrol guys. "Drive where? There's nothing out here. This is just a county road off the interstate."

"Shut up. Keep driving."

Behind me the other Humvee pulled out of the convoy and headed in our direction. I knew they'd have to leave at least some of their guys behind to protect the Elderwood folks and presumably continue them on their evacuation route to the shelter in Nashville. I wondered who was coming to help *us*. I made a show of my bare toes slipping off the accelerator and wove on the road as I stretched my leg out again. "This is crazy, mister. The SWAT guys will have already contacted all the police around here and set up a roadblock. We'll be stopped before we go another quarter mile."

"Maybe not, lady," he replied. "The boss said he's got everybody focused on that little Podunk town back east of here. He doesn't figure anybody else is on the road except a sleepy mailman and a retired dog catcher."

When I slowed slightly, hoping it wouldn't be noticed, Tan Jacket's pistol nudged me again in the neck. "Faster."

We passed a road sign — Highway 171 and Mt. Juliet were four miles ahead. I had never been there but assumed it was even smaller than Verdeville. "Come on, mister," I said, sounding deliberately whiny, "this is idiotic."

"Tell it to the boss," he said, pointing with his pistol. "Pull over up there."

Ahead, on a large empty lot with a long-neglected partial foundation set back from the road, I saw two Chevy Suburbans — both painted silver. Same ones that had passed us just moments earlier. Looked brand new, and neither one had plates. *Uh-oh.*

"Like I said, he's been waiting for you." He jabbed my neck again. "Pull in. Over behind those wagons."

I spotted Largo, leaning against one of the vehicles. "So your boss found his way out from under that fountain?"

Tan Jacket cackled. "That's not the boss. That's *Joey* Largo."

"So who's the boss, then?"

"Joe's big brother." From the other Suburban stepped the man in the bad suit who'd left the play performance a moment before I had.

I gasped. Then my eyes slammed shut as I groaned, "*He's* your boss?"

"Anthony Largo. His friends call him Tony, but you'd better stick with Mister Largo."

"You know him, señora?" asked Viejo.
"He's the one who massacred the audience I was in."

CHAPTER 24

―⧫―

"FINALLY WE MEET again, Mizz Temple," said Anthony Largo in the chilly voice of a sadist welcoming a new, permanent guest to his dark and damp torture chamber. He pulled open the driver's door, yanked me out, and grabbed the Humvee's keys. Quickly poking his head inside, he added, "Nice. I like those extra seats in back."

"How do you know me?" I struggled to control my emotions, positive he was directly involved in the death of my friend Pamela, both of my guards, and countless other innocent victims.

He moved closer, clutched at the fabric near my neck and spoke directly into my face. "You were the one I was after."

Before I could inquire, or even question the wisdom of doing so, the senior Largo yelled at Tan Jacket, "Tie up the SWAT guy and toss him in the way back. And who's that in the middle seat?"

"Just a harmless cripple," replied Tan Jacket.

Big Largo made some calculations. "For now, we'll keep him with us."

The younger Largo struggled with another body from one of the silver vehicles. A female, in uniform. Presumably still alive, but not moving on her own. The admiral! Thank God she wasn't dead, but she couldn't stand up.

Tan Jacket went over and helped carry her toward us.

"What did you do to her?" I screeched.

"Nothing, really," replied Anthony. "Haven't had time. You wouldn't believe the trouble we had sneaking out of town."

"Let me see her," I said, trying to sound like I was a nurse. "Why isn't she moving?"

"That explosion shook her up a bit. If the room had been a little smaller we wouldn't have had to waste so much ammo finishing off the others."

I checked the admiral's pulse and respiration. One was faint, the other shallow. But she was alive and it did not appear they had molested her. Yet. "What did you want with this Navy officer?" Her nametag said *PEETE*.

"Nothing, really. Like I said, she was a bonus after we let you slip through our fingers."

"Okay," I said, wondering why he tried to kill me in that explosion if he wanted to *get* me. I hoped it would help our situation to keep him talking. "Why would a drug cartel boss want me, for that matter?"

"Drug cartel?" He laughed until he started coughing. "You hear that, little brother? They fell for that idiotic cover story. What a bunch of morons."

I kept my mouth shut. In the distance, out of the corner of my eye, I saw the other Humvee approach, but it only pulled as far as the highway shoulder and stopped. Our rescuers.

Both of the Largo brothers also spotted it. "Keep these hostages in front of us and we'll be good to go." With Joey behind the admiral, Anthony behind me, and Tan Jacket behind our Humvee, that left two other thugs, who circled the second Suburban around in front of the grouping. Both of them, still in prison orange, got out and stood near us. The wagons were circled — well, horse-shoed.

"What's your plan here, Largo?" I asked. "You were better off in the annex building with a shrill federal negotiator yelling at you through her megaphone."

"No, we left some chumps there with a few low-value hostages, but we've got the two aces." Then he cackled deeply. "Well, maybe they'd think of you as queens — admiral and lieutenant governor. You think the public would ever forgive the feds if they do something stupid and force us to kill two high-ranking *women*?"

He had a point. "So if this isn't about a drug cartel getting their kingpin out of prison, what *is* going on? Why all this elaborate, high-profile, two-bus breakout?"

He paused and winked at Joey. "Had to get my little brother out of the pen... and this was the first, last, and only time they were likely to move him. All those other creeps were just a bonus."

I strained to see if Viejo was tuned in to this conversation, but my view was partly blocked. I thought I saw him making a face at me, but it didn't translate. So I refocused on Largo. "And the bombs and weapons?"

"Diversions to get the feds to focus on the shock and awe while Joey settled accounts with that old biddy who ratted on him." Then he nudged his brother. "Did you fix that stoolie so she can't testify any more?"

"Never got a chance, man," said Joey with obvious disgust. "She went and died before I could get to her."

I could only imagine what Joey would have done to poor old Mrs. Pollard. "And killing all the audience members and those young actors?"

"Couldn't be helped."

I swallowed hard. "And Denny and Todd were also just pawns to be destroyed?"

Anthony looked puzzled. "Oh, your bodyguards. No. They were threats. Had to be eliminated."

I whipped around and clawed at his face.

He staggered away and then slugged me backhanded. My short nails hadn't done any real damage, but he *was* startled.

I dropped to the hard, gravelly ground, too angry to cry. My face felt like I'd smacked into a cement block wall. Hazily, I saw movement at the distant Humvee but still didn't know who'd arrived in it or what they intended.

"Your gallant rescuers are itching to do something," said Anthony.

"They're going to zoom in here and hack out your hearts with a pickaxe," I said, wondering where I'd dredged up that imagery and why I'd dared verbalize it. Admiral Peete finally stirred and I lurched down beside her.

Her mouth was moving. "Water," she whispered.

"This lady needs medical attention," I said. "There should be some water in that Humvee." I stood to go check.

"Naw. You stay here." Then he motioned to Tan Jacket. "See if they have any water."

Tan Jacket scampered around the front of the Humvee.

"Where's your phone?" he asked me.

"In my purse."

"And bring me her purse. It's time for her phone call to the cops out there."

"Okay, boss."

Through the open window, I saw Viejo hand him a bottle. Then Tan Jacket tucked his own pistol into his belt and quickly returned with the water in one hand and my purse in the other. "She must carry bricks in here," he said, tossing it to Anthony.

I strained to ignore my purse and focused on the water. I wondered whether the Largo brothers had been properly trained never to poke around inside ladies' handbags.

"Keep an eye on that old guy," instructed Joey, finally attempting to assert some leadership.

After Anthony nodded his assent, Tan Jacket opened the driver's door and perched on the edge, beside the seat, where he could monitor Viejo. Apparently not too worried about a handicapped senior citizen, the thug kept his pistol under his belt.

Adm. Peete slowly opened her eyes. It was obvious she wasn't seeing clearly, but she seemed to be able to tell I was not a convict. "What? Where?"

The two silent, orange-clad convicts sat inside the Suburban on the floor, with the sliding door open toward us. Casually smoking cigarettes, they incongruously appeared as though it were a normal day trip outside their prison walls.

"Shh. Here's some water," I said. "Just take a little bit and lie down and rest." I wanted her low for several reasons.

"You got a number for whoever's in charge of your friends out there?"

"It's probably the SWAT captain or lieutenant. I don't know either number, but you can get it if you call the capitol and speak with the intern who's running the switchboard right now."

"I'm not calling directory assistance," said Anthony with clear disgust. "You call the intern. But get that SWAT dude on the phone quick. He needs to know the ground rules... and that we're not bluffing."

"What are your stipulations?"

"You and the Navy chick go with us, in this captured Humvee. Anybody follows, we kill the old man. We drive down into Mississippi and disappear. My brother and I vanish and these three friends of ours take one of the silver trucks wherever they want to go."

"What happens to Viejo and me... and Admiral Peete?"

He shrugged. "Depends on whether anybody chases us and who they are."

In other words, as soon as we were no longer useful we were dead. "Help me get the admiral inside the Humvee. Viejo was a medic in the war." That was a lie. "And she needs to get out of this direct sunlight."

Neither Largo brother moved.

"You want your hostage dead before you get a chance to use her for leverage?"

At that, Anthony nodded to Joey, who came over and pulled Peete to her feet. I stayed in my crouch on the ground. "Okay, if he's taking care of her, I can make the call now."

He started to hand me the purse, but its weight clearly bothered him. "He said you had a brick in here. What is it really?"

"One of those older phones with a heavy charger unit, some makeup, and feminine, uh, hygiene products that wouldn't interest you," I replied, reaching up for my purse.

"Okay. Make the intern call real quick and keep it on speaker."

"No problem." Through the Humvee window, I looked up at Viejo and hoped he was ready. Couldn't tell. With the purse on the ground at my right, I pulled out the phone with my left hand and began punching buttons.

Anthony looked impatient. "Forget the number?"

"Forgot to enter the area code," I replied, and punched a few more numbers.

"Hey, wait a minute," he growled, "you're just stalling."

Way behind Anthony, I saw Lt. Staubach and Doc trotting our direction. A third person, unidentifiable at that range, had split away from them. I shifted my eyes at Viejo, hoping he'd look, but I couldn't tell if he'd read me.

"You'd better get your wannabe heroes on the horn," barked Anthony, "and make them stop."

My eye-pointing had alerted everybody, not just Viejo. Now all eyes were on Doc and Staubach jogging in our direction and less than a hundred yards away. Seeing the rescuers en route, the two orange-clad convicts jumped inside their Suburban, hurriedly cranked the engine, and peeled out... leaving a gap in the horseshoe of protection Largo had designed. Doc and Staubach ignored their departure and continued toward us.

Anthony cursed and stomped toward me, clearly planning to use me as his shield. But he paused half a second and said, "Joey, get this thing rolling. We're outta here."

With one rough hand on my collar, Anthony yanked me up from the ground. The phone fell, I whipped my pistol out of the purse, remembered it was cocked and locked and needed only the safety disengaged, aimed at Largo's face, and pulled the trigger.

Nothing.

CHAPTER 25

THE BERETTA DIDN'T fire? *Impossible.*

In the time it took Anthony to narrow his eyes and smile cruelly, Viejo had pulled his .38, shot Tan Jacket in the upper body, grabbed that criminal's pistol, and was aiming at the elder Largo through the open window. Joey dropped the admiral like a sack of horse feed and took off running toward the woods.

In that same second, I racked the slide, expelled an unfired cartridge, and fumbled again with the Beretta's safety, which I had only flipped halfway before. This time I aimed at Largo's chest.

But Largo, no longer clutching my collar and having backed up a mere step, had me point blank and he called over his shoulder, "Hey, old guy, if you twitch again in there, I'm gonna drop this governor lady in a bloody heap."

"Shoot him, Viejo," I yelled. I'd seen too many movies where the good guys put down their guns. It never ended well. "Shoot him!"

"Señora..."

Why it never dawned on me to pull my own trigger again, I'll never know. But when a panting Doc yelled from behind the remaining Suburban, "Julia, take him down!" I realized my fingers knew what to do but my brain hadn't given them permission.

When Largo turned toward Doc's voice, a rifle shot rang out. Largo's head exploded and simultaneously I blasted a hole in his chest. His body lurched grotesquely and crashed to the ground. Buckets of blood and gore, but not a subsequent twitch.

Then I collapsed, staring at my pistol. Doc, out of breath, hustled over to me and pried the weapon from my hands. Staubach approached the doubly-dead Largo like he was the rogue rhino on the final day of a large game safari. Poking Anthony's body with the barrel of his rifle, the lieutenant spoke on his collar radio, presumably to the captain, en route to Nashville by that point.

"Admiral Peete's in the Humvee," I managed to say, before I began sobbing as Doc held me tightly. "She's alive."

A THP cruiser streaked past us on the highway, heading toward the long-gone Suburban with the two convicts.

"Is that other guy armed?" Staubach asked Viejo.

"I lost track." The old man handed over Tan Jacket's pistol, butt first, with the magazine ejected. "But he ought to be easy to track down. Joey's soft and stupid."

After untying Billup in the back seat, the lieutenant used his mic to communicate with our third rescuer, evidently now pursuing Joey. "Sergeant Tuck will catch him. What did they do to the corporal?"

"Conked on the head with a pistol," I replied.

Then, indicating Peete, Staubach asked, "What's her condition?"

"I didn't see any blood," answered Viejo, "so I don't think she was hit by shrapnel, but the blast from a grenade in close quarters can knock the life out of you. Might be some internal problems... possibly busted eardrums."

"I've got an ambulance on the way," replied the lieutenant. "They'll get her to the nearest hospital. How about you?"

"They totally ignored me," said Viejo, a hint of sadness mixed with his relief. "To them, I was just an old man with shriveled legs. They never even checked my pouch."

"Their mistake. But Mister Rodriguez, I have to ask you," said the lieutenant slowly. "You had the better angle on our target. Why didn't you take the shot?" He said it like he was talking to a SWAT colleague who'd been on the same radio net with other sharpshooters.

Viejo sighed heavily and shifted his answer to me. "Señora, I knew I wouldn't miss hitting Largo, but in case he did have a split second to shoot you, I didn't want to be responsible for his finger pulling that trigger."

Staubach nodded, so he must have understood. In the SWAT business, they would often deal with that decision.

"Lieutenant, that was a good shot," added Doc. "How far away were you?"

"Way too close for a scoped rifle," he replied. "Had to use the iron sights. If I'd had any sense, I would've fired my pistol at that range. The captain will kill me when he finds out."

I knew none of us would spill the beans, but the ballistics would tell the tale. However, I needed more info. "So why did you risk that shot, lieutenant?"

"When he turned to look in Doc's direction, the barrel of his pistol wavered for an instant," replied Staubach. "That was my window."

"Who was that guy anyhow?" asked Doc as he pointed to the body. "He was at the play."

"Joey Largo's big brother, Tony."

CHAPTER 26

BEFORE I COULD explain any more, in a flurry of noise and movement, a TV sound truck — one of the Nashville stations — careened off the narrow highway and spit dirt and gravel as they stabilized in what would have been the sizeable front yard of this unfinished, isolated dwelling.

"What's going on out here?" yelled the driver. "We were on our way to Verdeville when we got re-routed." Clearly they'd already spotted the lieutenant governor, two SWAT vehicles, the SWAT-armed lieutenant in civvies, and were within a few feet of discovering the missing admiral. The media van quickly emptied.

There were only three of them — female reporter, camera guy, and male driver — but they seemed to be a swarm, firing a barrage of questions in multiple directions and not waiting for answers. Actually, among their rapid-fire quizzing, we learned a few things, like the two vans had been stolen from a new car lot in downtown Verdeville and had been seen heading west toward Nashville. TV teams had been sent on different routes to hopefully intercept them.

Wished I didn't have to deal with media right then, but I knew two things: One, Staubach, in civvies and from a unit that had not yet been activated, was where he wasn't supposed to be. And two, I was Tennessee's elected lieutenant governor and was expected to have enough executive savvy to stand up straight, tell the public and media what was what, and get on with business. Formerly, my guts would've protested that I was no more of an executive than a nineteen-year-old intern in my father's senate office. But in all the events of this afternoon, I'd finally crawled out of that cocoon.

I put my uncomfortable shoes back on, straightened my skirt and jacket, and made an ineffectual swipe at my errant hair. For my first impromptu media event since the election, I was a visual wreck. *Shrug it off... don't call attention to it.*

I didn't mention Verdeville, but there was no point in trying to float the governor's fantasy about me not being *here* — their tape was already rolling. I explained some Verdeville evacuees had been jumped by several escapees; the THP and other state law enforcement had responded bravely and efficiently. Admiral Peete, alive but worse for wear, had been rescued.

I told them the governor would be holding a press conference later that afternoon and no further statements would be made from this site. Then I got out of range of their microphones and called Ampersand to update him. He yammered about strategy and spin and message consistency.

"It's up to you to explain the involvement of the SWAT team, Governor."

He sputtered for scarcely a second. "So what are you going to do?"

"I'll still meet those two reporters before this evening's news, because if I cancel, it'll be even worse. And I'll just tell them, *on* the record, the broad outline of what happened during this whole bizarre experience."

"They'll demand more information and insist we prepare a complete statement."

"That's what your press team is for, Governor. I'll give you a detailed report in the morning." I mentioned Sgt. Tuck was hot on the trail of Joey Largo. "And you can get the rest of this portion from Lieutenant Staubach."

Ampersand wanted to protest a bit more, so I just handed my phone to the lieutenant and let them tussle.

A church bus rolled up, taking the turn off the highway as carefully as if they were carrying 300 loose eggs. Actually their cargo was fifteen seniors en route to bingo by way of a nearby buffet, it turned out — thirteen women with two men who strutted like potbellied roosters. Judging from the swanky van, this could only be the largest Catholic church in Mt. Juliet. The sixteenth person was a scrawny, middle-aged, male driver.

Some remained on the bus, while a few exited and milled around. Several of the group snapped phone photos, of the scene and of me, so there were now additional reasons my presence could not be erased. And suddenly I realized I didn't want myself whitewashed out of the afternoon's events. I would never have wished for those experiences, but now that I'd survived them, I sensed a measure of validation I couldn't recall feeling before.

Staubach called again for backup and did his best to prevent any incursion near either of the two wounded, Peete and Tan Jacket, and the bloody body of the elder Largo. I hadn't seen even a flash of Sgt. Tuck, so evidently Joey Largo was more elusive than we'd assumed.

Viejo was getting a lot of attention, mostly through the Humvee window, from both the reporter and a few of the church seniors. Also a practicing Catholic, he'd apparently hit an intuitive chord with them. Near him, in the back seat, Cpl. Billup was moaning and finally stirring.

Shortly a Greene County Sheriff's Department cruiser arrived, with about as much ruckus as the media van had caused. Finally some backup, two deputies, to contain the scene. Staubach briefed them and got one of them to help carry Viejo from the Humvee to the front passenger seat of the abandoned Suburban. For the moment, Admiral Peete remained stretched out on the Humvee's middle seat with Staubach hovering near.

Then Staubach came back over to me and with a somewhat sheepish expression said, "Ma'am, those deputies didn't want to tell you this, so they asked me to."

What now? I waited, patiently, shielding the sun from my eyes. "And?"

"It's about this Suburban. It's part of the crime scene. They're going to need to process it as soon as possible and have to preserve it in the meantime."

"I understand," I replied. "We won't bother anything."

The lieutenant started to respond, but Doc interrupted. "Can you tell the deputies that the lieutenant governor is invoking her special state executive priority to temporarily commandeer a useful property and waive its immediate use for the agency conducting the investigation of the part that property played in the crime which has just been committed?"

"Huh?" Staubach said it before I could.

"Just tell them it's part of that revised state constitution," continued Doc. "By the time they figure it out, we'll be long gone."

"You can't be serious."

"Look, Lieutenant," I said, as calmly as I could muster, "I'm dead on my feet. It's too hot; I've been scraped, hit, and shot at. I need to sit before I collapse and I'm not going to plop down in this gravel. Okay?"

Staubach turned, shaking his head, and began walking back toward the deputies. "Don't shoot the messenger," he muttered.

"Doc, what was all that baloney about my state executive priority?"

After smiling broadly, he winked. "Just don't touch anything you don't have to."

While the media folks, following my firm closing announcement, had finally left me alone, a few of the church seniors approached to snap a photo or ask if I was okay. I begged them not to take pictures, and at least one of them said she'd voted for me. The bus driver pulled around a bit, presumably so they could be in better shade, but also, I suspected, because it afforded the passengers on his side a better view of me and Viejo in the Suburban.

I was slumped in the Suburban's middle seat. The dealership in Verdeville had already been notified, I was told, and would reclaim it from the impound facility after it was processed. But for the moment, it was (at that section of Highway 171) the most comfortable spot which didn't have somebody's blood and guts splattered everywhere. The driver's seat of the Humvee was plastered with gore from Tan Jacket, who miraculously was still breathing.

In addition to being completely exhausted, I felt stunned and a bit light-headed.

Doc could tell and he handled me like a fragile, precious sculpture. "If this is about dispatching Largo, you can't let it get to you." He swallowed hard. "He was half a second from killing you when Staubach nailed him."

"But I shot him, too." I'd never shot anything bigger than a rabbit and I hadn't enjoyed that. "Today I killed a man."

Doc's hands opened and closed like he was searching for his lines in a script. "He was dead when the lieutenant's 5.56-millimeter bullet penetrated his skull. If it lets you sleep better, you just fired at a dead man."

I didn't feel any better at all.

"That was the guy who set the blast in the performance. He was obviously a hardened criminal who'd probably spent much of his own life in prison. But he had no conscience whatsoever. Killing and maiming and taking hostages was just an afternoon's work for him. I don't guess you need reminding that one of your troopers, after being shot, also took a close-range round to the head. If that wasn't Largo himself, he'd certainly ordered it."

Why'd he have to mention Todd and Denny again? "I know, I know. I understand. Largo got what he deserved…"

"And no telling whatever else he had planned for you and the admiral."

"Yeah, I get all that. But all that death and destruction. Was it really just about breaking his little brother out of jail?"

Doc shrugged. "I thought it was something about a drug cartel."

Then I explained what Largo had said about targeting me.

"Seems like the proverbial sledgehammer to kill a flea." Then he reconsidered. "Or catching catfish with dynamite."

I didn't care about the imagery. "What did Largo hope to gain by bringing us way out here?"

"The farther away from all that downtown mess, the better," Viejo ventured a guess. "With two hostages, maybe he figured he held all the cards, señora."

Doc nodded. "But it turns out he had to fold."

So much remained confusing and I still needed answers — especially about how I fit in. "None of this makes sense. I just set out this morning to watch a few play selections in a little town and catch up with a sorority friend."

"Did Largo offer any explanation?" asked Doc.

"Not really. He said I was his original hostage target, so evidently he knew I'd be there." I shuddered. "And that's really creepy."

Doc hugged me tighter. "It's over now. You're safe. We've got the admiral back. Without a convict leader at the annex, the feds will talk those remaining guys out pretty easily, I'd bet."

"Why would I have shown up on Largo's radar at all?" Then a light flickered on. "Unless he had some beef with my late dad and figured to take it out on me."

"Do U.S. senators have much to do with prisons?" asked Doc.

"Possibly. He was on hundreds of Senate committees."

"More of that misplaced Largo payback," suggested Viejo.

After carefully unwrapping his arm from my shoulders, Doc climbed out of the Suburban and stood in the doorway, holding my nearer hand in both of his. "I don't know all the whys, Julia, but at least there's one good purpose to all this." He didn't wait for me to inquire. "I've found you again." Then he made a noise between a grunt and a sigh and trudged back toward the distant Humvee in which he'd arrived.

We heard sirens in the distance, so hopefully that was medical assistance headed our way for Adm. Peete, Cpl. Billup, and whatever they could do for the wounded Tan Jacket.

"They'll probably take your revolver, Viejo," I said, likely sounding like a detached observer rather than an integral participant in one long afternoon.

"Maybe so, señora, but I'll get it back eventually. And at least I put it to good use."

"Well, thanks for, um…"

"I had to neutralize the jacket guy or he might've shot you."

I understood… just couldn't verbalize it.

"You know," said Viejo suddenly, "Doc's right."

CHAPTER 27

———⁕———

DOC'S RIGHT ABOUT what? "Beg your pardon?"

"About the good part of all this — you two meeting again." He nodded in the direction Doc had gone. "Go ahead, señora. I think he's one worth holding onto."

"He's not truly interested in me, Viejo. He's just remembering a teenaged crush."

Viejo shook his gray head. "You don't really believe that."

But I knew I should. "He basically saved my life today... getting me out of that annex. Not to mention that he was willing to stay at Elderwood with all of us and help out." I took a deep breath. "But in a few minutes we'll be going our separate ways. Just passing ships."

Viejo smiled softly.

"Do you know something I don't?"

"Maybe I do." And he waited a five-count before explaining. "Earlier today, Doc asked me if a regular citizen could date a lieutenant governor."

I guess I'd wondered about that also. "For real?"

"I heard it with my own eyes."

"What the heck does that mean, anyhow?" I asked. "You said it earlier."

"Oh, something my grandmother used to say, only she said it in Spanish. Her version was considerably more colloquial, but you could roughly translate it this way: *Yo no sólo lo vi, pero también escuché.* I not only saw it, but also heard it."

"Puzzling expression." *But back to the earlier matter.* "So what did you tell Doc? About, um, dating, I mean." My heart raced as I waited for his answer.

The old man grinned and paused so long I was ready to pinch him. "I told him, sure, if he's a registered voter."

"I forgot to ask. Is he?"

"Señora, people of my age believe some things are best left for the young lovers to work out themselves."

"Lovers?"

"Well, in the sense of a storybook. You know, *boy meets girl.*"

I mulled that over. Wondered if *girl got boy* by the end of this story. "Anyhow, I've only known him since around noon."

"Maybe so, but you saw more of the real person in these few hours than you would in several months of casual contact with anybody else. You know what Doc Holliday is made of." Viejo paused to scratch a spot on his jaw. "And just as important, he learned a whole lot about you."

Evidently Doc and the old man had held quite a conversation at some point, so I asked Viejo several more questions. I was startled at how much territory they'd covered.

As I sat in the Suburban, wondering how long before the authorities would impound it, I silently calculated where the convoy of evacuees likely was by now. For the folks from Elderwood, it was a deliverance from peril... and, presumably, in a day or two they could return to their own rooms. Britney would likely be picked up by a family member within an hour. Viejo would be soon transported to the shelter with the rest of his co-residents.

But what about me? What about Doc? We had so little time left.

Assuming a new THP cruiser would arrive shortly to pick me up and convey me to my apartment, as Staubach had mentioned, I would have hardly more than an hour left to change clothes, make some pretense of arranging my hair, and then ride with a new security team to the newspaper office to spill my spiel. Then I'd return home to my empty dwelling, phone the next of kin for both Todd and Denny, cry with them, and ponder the long day — one eye glued to the news and praying for the remaining hostages.

Doc re-approached the Suburban after driving the Humvee up beside us. Despite being clearly exhausted, he was still a handsome specimen, albeit sweaty and considerably rumpled. He'd been wonderful all day. Didn't know how I would've made it without someone like him. Without *him*. But what would Doc Holliday do after I was gone and he answered a few questions from either the deputies or someone higher up? Unless it had been stolen or destroyed by now, his truck was still in downtown Verdeville's war zone, somewhere in a parking lot south of the embattled annex. When could he get back to his vehicle? How else could he return home to Clarksville?

Most importantly: after all this, would I ever see Doc again?

He smiled broadly as he held up a bag. "Had to go back for your snacks. Got your favorite, I hope."

"You remembered my snacks?" No way he could guess my favorite of anything. We hadn't known each other long enough even for me to learn his real first name. Why was this brave, resourceful, supportive man even registering on my radar? And why couldn't I discern what type of signature his blip created on my screen? "Thank you, Doc. I'm sure it will be lovely."

Viejo cleared his throat. "Under normal circumstances, señora, I'd wheel myself out of your way and give you two some privacy. But..." He pointed down to the slack khaki covering his shriveled legs.

"It's okay." I gripped his strong shoulder.

Doc handed Viejo a cola. After giving me another one and a candy bar, he looked at me with puzzlement on his wrinkled brow.

I re-checked my watch. "We don't have much time, Doc." I thought about removing my heels, but I don't do well with bare feet on gravel. "Let's take a walk."

"Don't go far," warned Staubach, just then approaching in a trot past the church bus. "Highway patrol will be here for you in four minutes."

I waved my acknowledgement and stepped out of the Suburban. This was important and we needed more than 240 seconds alone to discuss it, but I'd certainly learned one lesson that afternoon — time would not stretch just to suit us. Well, to suit me. I still didn't know if "us" actually existed and, if so, what "we" even wanted.

Doc sensed my mood, if not my worry. "It's been a crazy afternoon."

So much confusion, so little time. "Doc, I have a million questions."

He looked taken aback. "For example?"

"What you do for a living, why you moved to Clarksville, why you broke off your engagement..."

"How did you know...?"

"Viejo told me earlier," I answered. "But I think I've got a year's worth of questions and we have only a few fractured minutes left to, um, be together." Three minutes, to be exact.

He appraised me as though I had just emerged from a space ship and he needed to classify my species. "This isn't complicated, Julia. It took me fourteen years to find you again and I don't plan to let you go until one of us comes up with a good reason to be apart."

Huh? That sounded pretty forward. "How are you going to get your truck?"

He shrugged. "Nobody will be allowed in that disaster setting for at least a couple days, so I guess I'm stranded 'til I can rent something."

He made it sound ordinary to have your vehicle overtaken by escaped convicts and impounded by federal authorities. I wondered how he'd fill out the insurance paperwork. A thousand other puzzlements had me paralyzed. "But what about all my questions?"

"Let the answers come slowly. No need to rush."

"But by the time those state troopers drive me to my apartment, I'll have less than an hour to change clothes, collect my new security team, and rush to my appointment..."

"Relax. We have plenty of time." He smiled. "I'll go with you."

"You'll what?"

"Heck, I've been following you around Verdeville — and now some part of west Greene County — for hours, so why not?" Then he stared at his dusty boots for a moment. "Besides, I have some questions for you, too."

Wondered what they were. "But I have to wrestle with those reporters."

"I know. But they'll have a lobby — right? I'll read a magazine while you're setting them straight. Then we'll get rid of your guards, jump in your car, and find a quiet place to get some supper."

Supper? "Uh, that almost sounds like a date." Two minutes until my departure.

He reached for my hand and held it tenderly. "It's not complicated, Julia. Step of faith. One pace at a time. All you have to decide right now is whether you'd like a companion for supper."

Over Doc's shoulder, I saw Lt. Staubach shooing back on board the Catholic seniors who'd exited their bus. "We're almost out of time, Doc."

Then he suddenly hugged me. Not so tightly that I couldn't breathe, but snugly enough that I dropped the candy bar and nearly lost control of my beverage. "No, we're not, Julia. Time starts over. We've reset the game clock."

I was talking to a stranger I'd just met and he acted like we were about to begin a new life together. "What do you mean?"

"There's no rush. We have all the time we need." He rested his chin upon my head and breathed in deeply. "You'll have time to learn whatever you want to know about me and we can both take our time."

"One minute, ma'am," yelled Staubach. He had to be in radio contact with the approaching THP cruiser... and his watch had to be fast besides.

Time is relative. "You mean you'll go with me to my apartment, stick around while I change clothes and meet my new security guys, then accompany me to the interview, and still wait for me?" I had to repeat it because Arnold Bane had never wanted to delay an extra second on my behalf. "And later we go to supper?"

He nodded.

Sometimes my pragmatic side just swoops in and tries to ruin everything. "But what happens afterwards?"

He moved his chin from the top of my head and pulled back enough to look into my eyes. "You really don't know?"

I hadn't dated anybody in the thirty months since I'd split up with Arnold. All I could do was gulp and repeat, "No, what happens after we dine?"

"Dessert." As he lightly kissed my lips, a cheer rose up from the engrossed bingo Catholics. "We seem to have crowd approval," said Doc. "That should count for something, at least in politics."

"That's it, folks," yelled Staubach, apparently rushing real time. Then he pumped his arm up and down. "Ma'am, your ride is here."

So much had happened so quickly. My exhaustion, confusion, and lack of relationship equilibrium had suddenly created a sense of giddiness. "How can I make an executive decision about something this important, Doc? That wasn't even a real kiss."

"Maybe not, Julia," he said with a warm smile. "But it's taken fourteen years to get this close to you. I think I can wait another couple of hours for a real kiss."

Something warm glowed deep inside me — my arms inside the wool-blend jacket sleeves were covered with goose bumps. What on earth was I contemplating? "I haven't had all those years you've had to think about this, Doc. Can you be patient while I try to catch up?"

His reply was a kiss. A real one. Deep and warm and intense — it weakened my knees and took away my breath. Another cheer rose from the bingo-bound seniors in the church bus.

From the nearby Suburban, Viejo yelled out, "And I heard it with my own eyes!"

"Time's up, ma'am. These vehicles are about to be impounded and your ride is here," yelled the irritating, time-conscious lieutenant, on his way to brief the approaching THP officers. "Let's head 'em out."

Attempting to ignore the ecclesiastical peanut gallery, I pulled back, tried to catch my breath, and then embraced Doc tightly. "I thought you said you'd wait for that kiss."

"Changed my mind, Julia Temple," he said with a warm, low rumble in his voice. "Couldn't wait any longer after all." Then he picked me up like a new bride and carried me to the waiting THP cruiser.

– 30 –

AUTHOR'S NOTE

―――⸻―――

AS I WAS writing this story, I viewed it as a companion piece (or a "bookend") to another fast-paced tale set in my fictional town of Verdeville, Tennessee — *One Simple Favor*, released by Dingbat Publishing in 2015.

But I thought it might interest readers to learn the concept for this story arose directly from a dream I had on Nov. 26, 2014. I recalled very little of that dream — chiefly these few sentences:

I was part of the audience for a small presentation of selected portions of a play production. Most visible in that audience was a one-star admiral in full uniform. I was wearing the Ike jacket. Before the performance began, there was some cordial chit chat and somebody asked me about my jacket. I explained about the hash marks (one for each six months overseas).

Though most other people in the cast and audience were faceless, three of the performers were ladies. I observed something about the interaction among those three actresses in costume, but (on awaking) I didn't recall what it was.

As you can see, rather little of this dream made it to my short novel. But I immediately realized the key images — admiral, Ike jacket, play production — could be used in a story.

I typed up about 1100 words that same morning, just so I'd remember the dream-inspired concept, but had to leave it alone for seven months. At the end of June 2015, I dusted off this undeveloped story concept and knocked out some 22,000 words over eleven writing days. Had to break off for several external reasons, and during this time, I watched a few episodes of the TV series *24*, which my son had just given me. Viewing that very time-conscious show, I decided I'd like to condense the action of my story into a period of about one hour — just to see if I could. If so, it would be (in terms of duration) the fastest-moving story I'd ever written. [*I later realized — thanks to the perceptive eye of my content editor — my story actually consumes a period closer to about three hours.*] On July 27, a month or so later, I resumed work in earnest and after eight more writing days, I had a first draft which was essentially complete.

Over the subsequent months, when other projects and deadlines allowed, I continued to revise three additional drafts.

In early spring of 2016, I submitted the fourth draft to my publisher, who expressed interest but rightly suggested several significant changes. I made those and resubmitted the fifth draft, which was accepted on a tentative schedule for the autumn. Unforeseen events, not related to my manuscript, kept it on hold for nearly two years. Later, I transmitted the seventh draft which is the one we used to begin edits.

And that's how I came to experiment with a story which occupies only slightly more "real" time than it takes for you to read it.

ACKNOWLEDGEMENTS

This is my fourth venture with the talented Gunnar Grey at *Dingbat Publishing*. She continues to teach me subtleties of writing and editing as her keen eye and firm hand guide my manuscript toward publication. I am extremely grateful for the many ways in which she has aided my fiction career.

My long-time beta reader — my own brother and fellow author, Charles A. Salter — once again read my story promptly and (as usual) offered considerable helpful feedback. My wife, Denise Williams Salter, also read an early draft and provided several helpful observations.

Thanks to my friend, Kathy Heere Watts, for her research and assistance with the way Tennessee actually handles the office of the lieutenant governor. [*My story invents a state constitutional amendment which allowed my character, Julia Temple, to be elected directly to the office.*]

It was a pleasure to work again with the perceptive and thorough content editor Kay Springsteen Tate, who was also editor for the first of my sixteen published titles (and other manuscripts along the way).

Cover artist for this novel was also the talented Gunnar Grey.

ABOUT THE AUTHOR

Romantic comedy and romantic suspense are among thirteen completed novel manuscripts and four completed novellas. So far (with this novel), sixteen of these seventeen titles have been published and there are many more stories on the way.

I'm co-author of two nonfiction monographs (about librarianship) with a royalty publisher, plus a signed chapter in another book and a signed article in a specialty encyclopedia. I've also published articles, book reviews, and over 120 poems; my writing has won nearly forty awards, including several in national contests. As a newspaper photo-journalist, I published about 150 bylined newspaper articles and some 100 bylined photos.

I worked nearly thirty years in the field of librarianship. I'm a decorated veteran of the U.S. Air Force (including a remote tour of duty in the Arctic, at Thule AB in N.W. Greenland).

I'm the married parent of two and grandparent of six.

ALSO BY J. L. SALTER

Released by *Dingbat Publishing*:
"Double Down Trouble" (June 2018)
"One Simple Favor" (May 2015) — a novella
"Scratching the Seven-Month Itch" (September 2014)
"Curing the Uncommon Man-Cold" (December 2013)

Through *Clean Reads*:
"The Duchess of Earl" (July 2016)
"Pleased to Meet Me" (October 2015) — a novella
"The Ghostess & MISTER Muir" (October 2014)
"Hid Wounded Reb" (August 2014)
"Don't Bet On It" (April 2014) — a novella
"Echo Taps" (June 2013) — a novella
"Called to Arms Again" (May 2013)
"Rescued By That New Guy in Town" (October 2012)
"The Overnighter's Secrets" (May 2012)

With *TouchPoint Press*:
"Not Easy Being Android" (February 2018)
"Size Matters" (October 2016)
"Stuck on Cloud Eight" (November 2015)

ALSO FROM J.L. SALTER

PROLOGUE

Sunday, 10:12 p.m.

MY STOMACH GRUMBLED as I exited the gas station's restroom. I considered purchasing a candy bar, but then figured Aunt Mary would have ready a hearty stew or some other dish she could easily keep warm. So instead my next stop was the coffee machine, not far from a loud argument between a hostile man and a crying woman. But I tuned it out — plenty of travelers bicker when they're stressed from the road.

Then, out of the corner of my eye, I noticed Mike intently studying the entire scene.

Suddenly the angry man whacked the woman with a backhand. She yelped and added a combination of cursing and pleading to her sobs. Before I'd finished pouring my coffee, the man was roughing her up even more — shoving and yelling.

Being in the middle of a public nocturnal domestic dispute was the last thing I wanted, so I tried to signal Mike it was time to leave. But he'd moved from his former spot near the overpriced chips and stood about four feet from angry, violent Fisty and his cringing, crying girlfriend.

I even tried waving, but nothing I did registered at all — Mike's complete attention was on the aggressive brute. I figured my cousin-in-law was about two seconds from getting clobbered himself.

Then I heard Mike. Not the actual words initially — just his strong, firm, authoritative voice speaking to the man.

Whatever Mike said evidently got the attacker's attention, because Fisty dropped the woman like a limp blanket and whipped around. "What'd ya say?"

"I said leave her alone... back away. This isn't the time or place... or the proper handling of whatever's bothering you."

"You want me to show ya some proper handling?" asked Fisty. And he unleashed a haymaker that would've decked Muhammed Ali.

With a blur of sidestep and arm motion, Mike deflected that blow and instantly kung fu'd a maneuver that put the creep face down on the floor, with his arm twisted high behind his back and Mike's knee pressed sharply between his shoulders.

I dropped my coffee.

Scalding liquid splashing to the floor barely registered, because I was in shock. I'd need super slow mo and a rewind button to figure out all of Mike's moves, but my heart pounded and I thought I might faint. Hadn't felt that way since a live concert with Justin Timberlake...

#

Thanks for reading! Dingbat Publishing strives to bring you quality entertainment that doesn't take itself too seriously. I mean honestly, with a name like that, our books have to be good or we're going to be laughed at. Or maybe both.

If you enjoyed this book, the best thing you can do is buy a million more copies and give them to all your friends... erm, leave a review on the readers' website of your preference. All authors love feedback and we take reviews from readers like you seriously.

Oh, and c'mon over to our website:

www.DingbatPublishing.ninja

Who knows what other books you'll find there?

Cheers,

Gunnar Grey,

publisher, author, and Chief Dingbat

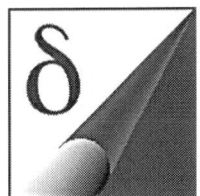

Made in United States
Orlando, FL
09 February 2024